NEW YORK REVIEW BOOKS
CLASSICS

THE STONE FA

WILLIAM GARDNER SMITH (1927–1974) was born and raised in a black working-class neighborhood of South Philadelphia, where his youth was punctuated by brutal episodes of racist violence: at fourteen, he was stripped and beaten by the police, and at nineteen was assaulted by a group of white sailors. A star student and passionate reader, Smith began reporting for the black-owned *Pittsburgh Courier* as a high-school senior and took a job at the paper after graduating at the age of sixteen. In 1946, he was drafted into the army and stationed in Germany; there he completed his first novel, describing a romance between a German woman and a black American soldier, which would be published two years later as *Last of the Conquerors*. Returning to the States, Smith continued to contribute to the *Courier*, studied at Temple University, led demonstrations against police brutality, and pursued an interest in Marxism that soon attracted the attention of the FBI. In 1949 he married Mary Sewell, and in 1950 he published his second novel, *Anger at Innocence*. Feeling stifled by racism and McCarthyism, Smith left for Paris, where he worked for Agence France Presse and became acquainted with Richard Wright and Chester Himes. His third novel, *South Street*, about a black radical who returns from exile in Africa to his hometown of Philadelphia, was met with little fanfare when it was published in 1954. In 1956, the US government declined to renew Smith's passport. Now divorced, he continued to live and work in France, where he met his second wife, Solange Royez, a teacher whose mother had escaped Nazi Germany, and in 1963 *The Stone Face* came out. Invited to help launch the first television station in Ghana, Smith moved in 1964, with his wife and infant daughter, Michèle, to Accra. His son, Claude, was born there, but after a military coup brought down the government of Kwame Nkrumah, the family returned to Paris. In France, Smith met and married his third wife, Ira Reuben, and another child, Rachel, was born. In 1967, he revisited the United States to write his final book, *Return to Black America*, published in 1970. He died of cancer in 1974 in a suburb of Paris.

ADAM SHATZ is the US Editor of the *London Review of Books* and a contributing writer to *The New York Times Magazine*, *The New York Review of Books*, and *The New Yorker*, among other publications.

THE STONE FACE

WILLIAM GARDNER SMITH

Introduction by
ADAM SHATZ

NEW YORK REVIEW BOOKS

New York

THIS IS A NEW YORK REVIEW BOOK
PUBLISHED BY THE NEW YORK REVIEW OF BOOKS
435 Hudson Street, New York, NY 10014
www.nyrb.com

First published as a New York Review Books Classic in 2021.

Library of Congress Cataloging-in-Publication Data
Names: Smith, William Gardner, 1927–1974, author. | Shatz, Adam, writer of
introduction.
Title: The stone face / William Gardner Smith ; introduction by Adam Shatz.
Description: New York : New York Review Books, [2021] | Series: New York
Review Books classics
Identifiers: LCCN 2020043522 (print) | LCCN 2020043523 (ebook) | ISBN
9781681375168 (paperback) | ISBN 9781681375175 (ebook)
Classification: LCC PS3537.M8685 S76 2021 (print) | LCC PS3537.M8685
(ebook) | DDC 813/.54—dc23
LC record available at https://lccn.loc.gov/2020043522
LC ebook record available at https://lccn.loc.gov/2020043523

ISBN 978-1-68137-516-8
Available as an electronic book; ISBN 978-1-68137-517-5

Printed in the United States of America on acid-free paper.
10 9 8 7 6 5 4 3 2 1

INTRODUCTION
A Stranger in Paris

IN 1951, in an essay entitled "I Choose Exile," the novelist Richard Wright explained his decision to resettle in Paris after the war. "It is because I love freedom," he declared, "and I tell you frankly that there is more freedom in one square block of Paris than there is in the entire United States of America!" Few of the black Americans who made Paris their home from the 1920s to the civil rights era would have quarreled with Wright's claim. For novelists such as Wright, Chester Himes, and James Baldwin, for artists and musicians such as Josephine Baker, Sidney Bechet, and Beauford Delaney, Paris offered a sanctuary from segregation and discrimination, as well as an escape from American puritanism—an experience as far as possible from the "damaged life" that Theodor Adorno considered to be characteristic of exile. You could stroll down the street with a white lover or spouse without being jeered at, much less physically assaulted; you could check into a hotel or rent an apartment wherever you wished so long as you could pay for it; you could enjoy, in short, something like normalcy, arguably the most seductive of Paris's gifts to black American exiles.

Baldwin, who moved to Paris in 1948, two years after Wright, embraced the gift at first but came to distrust it, suspecting that it was an illusion, and a costly one at that. While blacks "armed with American passports" were rarely the target of racism, Africans and Algerians from France's overseas colonies, he realized, were not so lucky. In his 1960 essay "Alas, Poor Richard," published just after Wright's death, he accused his mentor of celebrating Paris as a "city of refuge" while remaining silent about France's oppressive treatment of its colonial subjects: "It did not seem worthwhile to me to have fled the native fantasy only to embrace a foreign one."* Baldwin recalled that when an African joked to him that Wright mistook himself for a white man, he had risen to Wright's defense. But the remark led him to "wonder about the uses and hazards of expatriation":

> I did not think I was white, either, or I did not *think* I thought so. But the Africans might think I did, and who could blame them?...When the African said to me, *I believe he thinks he's white*, he meant that Richard cared more about his safety and comfort than he cared about the black condition.... Richard was able, at last, to live in Paris exactly as he would have lived, had he been a white man, here, in America. This may seem desirable, but I wonder if it is. Richard paid the price such an illusion of safety demands. The price is a turning away from, ignorance of, all of the powers of darkness.

"Alas, Poor Richard," like Baldwin's famous critique of Wright's *Native Son*, was an exercise in self-portraiture, if

---

*One wonders if Baldwin read Wright's 1954 book on African independence struggles, *Black Power*, which contains a number of scathing criticisms of French colonialism: "It's a desperate young black French colonial who resolves to return to his homeland and face the wrath of white Frenchmen who'll kill him for his longing for the freedom of his own nation, but who'll give him the *Légion d'honneur* for being French."

not self-congratulation. By then Baldwin had come home to America and joined the civil rights struggle that Wright, nursing his wounds in his exile, preferred to observe from afar. But in his autobiographical story "This Morning, This Evening, So Soon," also published in 1960, Baldwin implied that he too might have ended up the butt of an African's joke if he had stayed. The narrator, a black expatriate reflecting upon his estrangement from the Algerian "boys I used to know during my first years in Paris," remarks that "I once thought of the North Africans as my brothers and that is why I went to their cafés." But while he "could not fail to recognize" their "rage" at the French, which reminds him of his own rage at white Americans, "I could not hate the French, because they left me alone. And I love Paris, I will always love it."

Perhaps because he was grateful to the city that had "saved my life by allowing me to find out who I am," Baldwin never gave us a novel about the "uses and hazards of expatriation." This achievement belongs, instead, to a long-forgotten writer three years his junior, William Gardner Smith, a Philadelphian who moved to Paris in 1951 and died there in 1974, at the age of forty-seven, of leukemia. A journalist by trade, Smith published four novels and one work of nonfiction. The most striking of his books—and his deepest inquiry into the ambiguities of exile—is *The Stone Face*, a novel set in Paris against the backdrop of the Algerian War. Long out of print—the hardcover edition goes for $629.99 on Amazon, roughly $3.00 a page—it was published in 1963, the same year as *The Fire Next Time*. If it lacks Baldwin's prophetic eloquence, it radiates a similar sense of moral urgency. But where *The Fire Next Time* reflects Baldwin's return to his native land, his reckoning with its defining injustice, *The Stone*

Face explores a black exile's discovery of the suffering of others: an injustice perpetrated by his host country, a place he initially mistakes for paradise.

Simeon Brown, the protagonist, is a young black American journalist and painter who begins to question France's self-image as a color-blind society as he witnesses the racism experienced by Algerians in Paris and becomes aware of their struggle for independence back home. At once a bildungsroman and a novel of commitment, *The Stone Face* resonates with contemporary concerns about privilege and identity, but its treatment of these questions is defiantly heterodox. Among the beneficiaries of privilege in the novel are Simeon's black expatriate peers, who refuse to support the Algerian struggle, partly because they're afraid of being expelled from France but also because they'd rather not be associated with a despised minority. They are not perpetrators of anti-Algerian racism, but they are passive bystanders, clinging to the inclusion they've been denied at home. *The Stone Face* is an antiracist novel about identity, but also a subtle and humane critique of a politics that is based narrowly on identity.

The Martinican poet Aimé Césaire famously imagined a gathering of the oppressed at the "rendezvous of victory," but in *The Stone Face* the West's victims—black, Arab, and Jew—are often bitterly at odds in their struggle for a place at the table. One of the Algerian characters explodes into an anti-Semitic tirade, accusing Algeria's Jews of being traitors to the national cause, worse than the colonialists themselves. Stung by this outburst, Simeon's Polish Jewish girlfriend, Maria, a concentration camp survivor, begs him to forget about race and the Algerian question and live a "normal" life, but unlike her, Simeon does not have the option (nor the desire) to fully disappear into whiteness. No one in *The*

Stone Face is impervious to intolerance or moral blindness. (In a somewhat clumsy metaphor, both Simeon and Maria are visually impaired: one of his eyes was gouged out in a racist attack; she is undergoing surgery to avoid going blind.) The title alludes to the hateful face of racism, and Smith suggests it lies within all of us.

Fighting the stone face, Simeon learns, is not simply a matter of defending one's own people, and sometimes requires actively breaking with them. By the end of the novel, he has repudiated "racial" loyalty to his black American brethren in favor of a more dangerous solidarity with Algerian rebels. In its embrace of internationalism, the novel argues powerfully that exile needn't be a delusional fantasy or a solipsistic flight from one's ethical obligations. What matters, what is ultimately "black," for Smith, is not a question of one's identity or location but of conscience, and the action it inspires.

Born in 1927, Smith grew up in South Philadelphia, in a black working-class neighborhood of one of the North's most racist cities. By the time he was fourteen he had already been stripped naked and beaten with a rubber hose by police officers who felt that "I lacked proper respect." At nineteen he was assaulted at a nightclub by a mob of white sailors who thought that his light-skinned date was a white woman.

A precocious student of literature, Smith read the same novelists as most aspiring writers in midcentury America: Hemingway and Faulkner, Proust and Dostoyevsky. Keen to begin publishing, he turned down scholarships at Lincoln and Howard to take a job at a black-owned newspaper, the *Pittsburgh Courier*. But what really set him on his course as a novelist was being drafted into the army. In the summer of 1946 Smith went to occupied Berlin as a clerk-typist with the 661st TC Truck Company. He spent eight months in Germany, and by August 1947 he had completed a draft of a novel, *Dark Tide over Deutschland*. Farrar, Straus & Company paid him five hundred dollars for the manuscript and published it in 1948 under the title *Last of the Conquerors*. A reviewer in *The New York Times* described the novel—the story of a love affair between a black soldier in Berlin and a German woman, with strong echoes of *A Farewell to Arms*—as "a revealing example of the tendency of minority groups ... to project themselves into a fantasy world in which they enjoy rights that are inherently, if not actually, theirs."

Yet the love between Hayes Dawkins and Ilse Mueller is no fantasy, even if it is endangered by the racism of the American army, which polices "fraternizing" between black soldiers and German women. To read *Last of the Conquerors* today is to grasp that it is out of such "fantasy worlds" that freedom is ultimately born. "I had lain on the beach many times," Hayes muses, "but never before with a white girl. A white girl. Here, away from the thought of differences for a while, it was odd how quickly I forgot it.... Odd, it seemed to me, that here, in the land of hate, I should find this one all-important phase of democracy. And suddenly I felt bitter."

More than any novel of its time, *Last of the Conquerors* captured the paradoxes of the black American soldier's experience in Europe. Hayes has come to the Old World as a "liberator," but he serves in a segregated army that, for all its talk of spreading democracy, has imported the racist practices of Jim Crow.* And like many of his fellow black soldiers, he has his first taste of freedom in the arms of a

---

*As James Q. Whitman has shown in *Hitler's American Model*, these practices were closely studied by Nazi jurists.

white German woman—and in a country that has slaughtered millions of people on racial grounds.

Hayes is keenly aware of his good fortune in Germany—and also of how strange and precarious it is: *"Wonder how many Negroes were lynched in the South this year.... Wonder how many Congressmen are shouting white supremacy.... Nice being here in Berlin. Nice being here in Germany where the Nazis were once rulers. Nice being so far away that I can wonder—but not be affected."* Once his affair with Ilse is discovered, however, his superiors in the army do everything they can to keep the lovers apart, working closely with former Nazis in the local *polizei* no less eager to separate "the races." Nor is this the only prejudice they share. "Men, I forgot," Hayes's white captain says one evening, during an after-hours drinking session, "there was one good feature about Hitler and the Nazis":

> We waited for the one feature. "'They got rid of the Jews." A bolt of tenseness landed in the room. You could not see or hear it, but you could feel it land. The German girls were especially struck.... "Only thing. Only good thing they did.... We ought to do that in the States.... Jews take all the money.... Take all the stores and banks. Greedy. Want everything. Don't leave anything for the *people*. Did it in Germany and Hitler was smart. Got rid of them. Doin' it now in the States. Take the country over and *Americans* ain't got nothing to say about it."

After returning to Philadelphia, Smith attended Temple University on the GI Bill, helped organize demonstrations against police brutality, and studied Marx. (His ties to

Communists and Trotskyists raised the suspicion of the FBI, which would keep a file on him for the next two decades.) He married a local woman, Mary Sewell; received a fellowship from Yaddo; and published a novel, *Anger at Innocence* (1950), a story about a love affair between a middle-aged white man and a white female pickpocket half his age. But for all his success, Smith felt suffocated by racism and McCarthyism, and feared, as he later told an interviewer on French television, that if he stayed in America he would end up killing someone. The Trinidadian Marxist C. L. R. James suggested that he try living in France and gave him Wright's address on the rue Monsieur le Prince in the Latin Quarter.

In 1951, the Smiths sailed to France. They moved into a tiny hotel room for $1.60 a night, until they could find an apartment. He found a job at Agence France Presse (AFP), profiled Wright for *Ebony*, and became a drinking companion of Chester Himes and the great cartoonist Ollie Harrington at the Café de Tournon, a haunt of black writers and artists near the Luxembourg Gardens. He published a new novel, *South Street* (1954), about a black American radical who has returned from exile in Africa. But the reviews were lukewarm, and he felt that he'd "come to a dead end" and no longer wanted to follow "the road of protest." He took a long hiatus from fiction, divorced, and met the woman who became his second wife, Solange Royez, a schoolteacher from the French Alps whose mother had fled Nazi Germany as a child. Marrying a Frenchwoman reinforced his self-perception as an exile. So did the scrutiny of the American government, which declined to renew his passport in 1956, shortly after a visit he had made to East Berlin. For the next few years he lived in Paris as a "stateless" person.

"Youth was the most outstanding characteristic of William Gardner Smith—youth and naïveté," Himes wrote. But courage was another. Most of the black American exiles in Paris adhered to the unspoken agreement with the French government that, in return for sanctuary, they would not intervene in "internal" affairs, above all the sensitive question of French rule in Algeria, which was officially considered a part of France and divided into three departments. As Richard Gibson, a member of the Tournon circle, recalled, "There was a lot of sympathy for the Algerian national struggle among the American writers, but the problem was, how could you speak out and still stay in France?"

Even before the war of independence broke out in November 1954, Smith wrote about the oppression of Algerians in France. In an article for the *Pittsburgh Courier*, he described sitting on the terrace of the Café de Flore and overhearing racist chatter about an Algerian rug-seller who'd passed by: "A bell rings somewhere in your head. Echo from another land. You finish your beer and go home, tired, to bed." As Edward Said has written, "Because the exile sees things both in terms of what has been left behind and what is actual here and now, there is a double perspective that never sees things in isolation.... From that juxtaposition one gets a better, perhaps even more universal idea of how to think, say, about a human rights issue."

Yet exile alone does not guarantee this "double perspective." It requires time, reflection, and, above all, vigilance, since— as Baldwin observed acidly, and perhaps unfairly, of Wright— the adoptive country's acceptance, and pleasures, can prevent it from forming. In *The Stone Face*, Smith chronicles the emergence of Simeon's double perspective in three briskly told parts whose titles suggest his shifting identities: "The Fugitive," "The White Man," and "The Brother." When Simeon arrives in Paris in the spring of 1960, he is a refugee from America's race war—the first physical detail Smith supplies is that he has only one eye. Haunted by the monstrous face of his attacker, a "stone face" disfigured by rage, with "fanatic, sadistic and cold" eyes, he is trying, at the novel's opening, to reproduce it on canvas, the "*un-man*, the face of discord, the face of destruction." This is, literally, art therapy: "I left to prevent myself from killing a man," he confesses.

At first, Paris enables Simeon to heal, as he rejoices in the disappearance of the color line and falls into the soft embrace of the black American expatriate scene. In swift, deft strokes, Smith sketches the geography of what the historian Tyler Stovall calls "Paris noir": the soul-food restaurant run by Leroy Haynes in Montmartre, the Tournon and Monaco cafés, the bookshop near Wright's apartment on rue Monsieur le Prince, the jazz clubs. Himes makes a cameo as the grouchy novelist James Benson, a "strange cat, a sort of hermit" who "disappears into his apartment with whatever girl he happens to be living with," and occasionally emerges to curse the white world and the American government. It's at the Tournon that Simeon first sees Maria, an aspiring actress determined to forget her childhood in the camps, where she was protected by a Nazi guard who took a twisted interest in her: "This child-role was a mask; there were nightmares inside her head." Smith tenderly describes the beginning of their love affair as a meeting of survivors in the city of refuge.

What shatters Simeon's idyll is his growing awareness that while he has fled the stone face in America, it is no less present in France—in the country where he's at last able to breathe freely. At first he's too happy to pay much attention to the headlines in the papers: MOSLEMS RIOT IN ALGIERS, FIFTY DEAD. But when he sees a man "with swarthy skin and long crinkly hair" pushing a vegetable cart, he wonders if he might be Algerian, and remembers how a group of white people in Philadelphia "had stared at him—and how he had stared back, sullen, defiant, detesting their nice clothes and leisure and lazy, inquisitive eyes." Soon after, Simeon gets into a scuffle with an Algerian man, and both of them end up in the back of a police wagon. Simeon notices that the sergeant addresses Hossein with the familiar *tu* while using the polite *vous* with him. While Hossein is locked up for the night, Simeon is released. "You don't understand," the police officer tells him. "You don't know how they are, *les Arabes*.... They're a plague; you're a foreigner, you wouldn't know."

The next day he runs into Hossein, who asks him, "Hey! How does it feel to be a white man?...We're the niggers here! Know what the French call us—*bicot, melon, raton, nor'af.*" One of Hossein's friends, Ahmed, an introspective young medical student from a Berber family in Kabylia, invites him to dinner the following evening. They hop onto a bus together:

> The further north the bus moved, the more drab became the buildings, the streets and the people.... It was like Harlem, Simeon thought, except that there were fewer cops in Harlem.... The men he saw through the window of the bus had whiter skins and less frizzly hair, but they were in other ways like the Negroes in the United States. They adopted the same poses: "stashing" on corners, ready for and scared of the ever-possible "trouble," eyes sullen and distrusting.

Noticing that Simeon's attention has wandered, Ahmed asks him, "Where are you?" "Home," he replies.

Yet the Algerians, to Simeon's disappointment, do not "break into smiles and rush to embrace him shouting: 'Brother!' They kept their distance, considering him with caution, as they would a Frenchman—or an American." The fact that he is "racially" black does not make him an ally in their eyes; he must prove himself first. In *The Stone Face*, whiteness is not a skin color or a "racial" trait; it is, rather, a synonym for situational privilege. Relinquishing it, Smith suggests, is a difficult process, especially for an oppressed man who's barely begun to enjoy it. In a pivotal scene, Simeon brings his Algerian friends to a private club that he could never have joined in America. People at other tables whisper as they enter; the host is chillier than usual: "To his own astonishment, Simeon felt uneasy. Why was that?" Perhaps "he was afraid of something. Of losing something. Acceptance, perhaps. The word made him wince. Of feeling humiliation again. For one horrible instant he found himself *withdrawing* from the Algerians—the pariahs, the untouchables!... Sitting here with the Algerians he was a nigger again to the eyes that stared. A nigger to the outside eyes—that was what his emotions had fled." An argument erupts between a white woman and one of Simeon's friends, but Simeon, shamed by his initial response, rallies to his friend's defense and feels, for the first time, "at one with the Algerians. He felt strangely *free*—the wheel had turned full circle."

Simeon's black friends at the Tournon frown upon his decision to disavow his privilege: they have no desire to place their security in France in jeopardy. "Forget it, man," one of them says. "Algerians are white people. They feel like white people when they're with Negroes, don't make no mistake about it. A black man's got enough trouble in the world without going about defending white people." Maria is even more alarmed by Simeon's deepening attachment to his Algerian friends, one of whom—to Simeon's horror—has expressed a violent suspicion of Jews in her presence. Why, she asks, can't he "simply accept happiness" instead of "seeking complications"? After all, he fled a life of racism in America; must he continue to fight it here? "Perhaps the Negro who might want to marry you might not be able to flee," he replies. "Not forever. Because of something inside…"

That "something inside" is Simeon's conscience, and Smith describes what causes it to stir with extraordinary precision, in a remarkably authentic description of the Algerian War's impact on the *métropole*. As Simeon is taken into the confidence of his Algerian friends, he learns of the existence of detention centers and camps inside France, and of a network of French supporters for the resistance, the so-called *porteurs de valises*, or baggage carriers. He meets two young women, Algerian survivors of French prisons, one of whom was tortured in front of her father and fiancé with electrodes applied to her genitals; the other raped with a broken champagne bottle. And in the last pages of the novel, Smith provides a wrenching account of the police massacre of Algerian protestors on October 17, 1961—the only one that exists in the fiction of the period. (The first French novel to broach the topic, Didier Daeninckx's *Meurtres pour mémoire*, was published in 1984.) Smith's French publisher told him it was "very courageous to have written the book, but we can't publish it in France." Unlike his other books, *The Stone Face*, his only novel set in Paris, has never been translated into French.

The October 17 massacre took place in response to a peaceful demonstration called by the National Liberation Front (FLN) to protest a curfew imposed on all Algerians in Paris. Its architect was the head of the Paris police, Maurice Papon, who had successfully concealed his involvement in the deportation of more than 1,600 Jews in Bordeaux during the war, and gone on to serve as the police prefect in the Constantinois region of Algeria, where he presided over the torture of rebel prisoners. The FLN had killed eleven policemen in the Paris region since August, and, at one of their funerals on October 2, Papon boasted that "for one hit taken we shall give back ten." Under his orders, the demonstration was brutally suppressed; hundreds of protesters were killed, some in the street that evening, their bodies thrown into the Seine; others were beaten to death inside police stations over the next few days.* As Smith writes, "Theoretically, French police charges were aimed at splitting demonstrations into small pockets, and dispersing the demonstrators; but it was clear that tonight the police were out for blood.... Along the Seine, police lifted unconscious Algerians from the ground and tossed them into the river." Simeon sees a woman with a baby being clubbed, punches the officer who's attacking her, and ends up, again, in the back of a police van. But this time one of the Algerians riding alongside him says, "*Salud, frère*"—"Hello, brother."

The original draft of *The Stone Face* ended with Simeon heading to Africa, as his Algerian friends have urged him. In the final version, Simeon decides that it's time to go home, where civil rights activists are "fighting a battle harder than

---

*In 1998, the French government acknowledged that a massacre had taken place but placed the death toll at "several dozen"; in *La Bataille de Paris*, Jean-Luc Einaudi estimates that 325 were killed. The most comprehensive study of the "battle of Paris," Jim House and Neil MacMaster's *Paris 1961: Algerians, State Terror, and Memory*, concludes that "a conclusive or definitive figure... will never be arrived at."

that of any guerrillas in any burnt mountains. Fighting the stone face." Some admirers of the novel have interpreted its conclusion as a regrettable failure of nerve, a retreat from the cosmopolitan solidarity it otherwise promotes—in Paul Gilroy's words, a "capitulation to the demands of a narrow version of cultural kinship that Smith's universalizing argument appears to have transcended." But there is another way of understanding Simeon's decision. The Algerian struggle has not only given him the courage to confront the stone face he fled; it has transformed his understanding of American racism by inscribing it in a wider history of Western domination. When Simeon refers to black Americans, he now calls them "America's Algerians."

A longing for home, if not Eden itself, is, of course, a recurring theme in the modern novel; Georg Lukács argued that the form itself is shaped by a sense of "transcendental homelessness" in a world abandoned by God. In *The Stone Face*, the world has been deserted not by a higher power but by justice, which humans alone can create: in its absence, "home is where the hatred is," in the words of Gil Scott-Heron. Yet the critics of *The Stone Face* have a point. Smith obviously agonized over his exile from America, which separated him not only from his family but from black America at a time of revolutionary upheaval. "I sometimes feel guilty living way over here," he wrote his younger sister, "especially when I hear about 'freedom marches' and the like." But he had little interest in moving back to a country he disliked "not only racially, but also politically and culturally." Instead he left his job at AFP and went to Ghana, where W. E. B. Du Bois's widow, Shirley Graham Du Bois, had invited him to help her launch the independent state's first television station. He flew to Accra in August 1964 with

Solange and their one-year-old daughter, Michèle, and moved into a big house on the sea provided by Kwame Nkrumah's government.

"For the first time in a long time I feel very useful!" he wrote his mother shortly after his arrival. "This country is going places—Nkrumah is a real African patriot, and he wants his country to develop fast. The people walk proud and tall." He met other prominent African American writers living in Accra, including Maya Angelou and Julian Mayfield, and spent an evening talking to Malcolm X when Malcolm swept into town in November, three months before his assassination. In those early days, Smith allowed himself to dream that he'd come back home. Sounding not unlike Simeon among the Algerians of northern Paris, he wrote that on the boulevards of Accra he "felt, sometimes, as though I were walking down a street in South Philadelphia, Harlem, or Chicago. These black people in their multicolored robes, with their laughter, with their rhythmic gait, were my cousins." In July 1965 he affirmed his bond with the African motherland when Solange gave birth to their son, Claude.

Smith's African dream, however, disintegrated even more rapidly than his Paris reverie. While the "visible signs of black sovereignty" in Nkrumah's Ghana still moved him, he saw that "the Black Power of Ghana" had "grave limitations." He also realized that "the idea of black American nationalists, summed up in the phrase, 'We are black, therefore we are brothers,' is incomprehensible in tribal societies where the hereditary enemies have, precisely, been black. For the Ibo of Eastern Nigeria, the Hausa of the North is a much more fearful, deadly and *real* adversary than the white-skinned men across the sea he will never sail." Early in the morning of February 24, 1966, he and Solange were awakened by gunfire. The army and the police had staged a coup against Nkrumah. When Smith arrived at his office, he was detained by a group of armed men and taken to a rebel-controlled police station. He and his family flew to Geneva that evening with all their belongings, before returning to Paris.

Not long after their return, Smith separated from Solange. He had fallen in love with a young Indian Jewish woman working at the Indian embassy, Ira Reuben, the daughter of a judge on the high court of Patna; they married as soon as his divorce was finalized. (Their daughter, Rachel, now a singer and actress, was born in 1971.) Restless as ever, he continued to travel for AFP. In the summer of 1967, he spent three weeks in Algeria and a month in the United States, where he saw his mother for the first time in sixteen years. This reporting became the basis of his book *Return to Black America* (1970), a fascinating study of the transformations among "America's Algerians." He interviewed not only Stokely Carmichael and other Black Power leaders but gangsters such as Ellsworth "Bumpy" Johnson, the king of the Harlem underworld, who reminded him of Ali La Pointe, an Algerian rebel who started out as a criminal in the casbah. Youth gangs, Smith wrote, were "becoming the hard core of the black nationalist movement.... The same thing... occurred with Algerian gangs... during the Algerian liberation struggle." He marveled at the confidence exhibited by young black people, their fearlessness in confronting white supremacy, even "the way they moved, the way they acted." But "the real change, the real revolution, was *inside*. These black youths with whom I talked from coast to coast were much more different from most people of my generation than we were from the generation of our fathers."

What had triggered this cultural revolution among young

black Americans, he argued, was the Second World War, when black soldiers like himself were

> uprooted from their tenant farms and ghettos and hurled across the ocean to do battle with white and yellow men in the name of freedom, democracy, and equality. The war opened up new horizons. Many black Americans came alive for the first time in the ruins of Berlin, the coffeehouses of Tokyo, the homes of Frenchmen or Italians. Members of a victorious army, they found respect and consideration for the first time—but from the former enemy!

Black America's revolution, he suggested, had been fueled not only by oppression but by the enlarged perspective and imaginative freedom that displacement and exile had afforded. Nothing less than a *"radical transformation of the surrounding white society itself,"* he concluded, could answer the revolution's demands for equality "in every sphere—political, economic, social, and psychological." Like Baldwin, who drew a similar portrait of the Black Power era in his 1972 essay *No Name in the Street*, Smith predicted that white America would do everything in its power to resist such a transformation.

Before his death in 1974, Smith proposed a novel he called "Man Without a Country," about (in the words of his widow, Ira Gardner-Smith) "a black American who lives in France, who also lived in Africa, and because of these three continents—which all become part of him—he ceases to belong anywhere." He could not find a publisher. But in *Last of the Conquerors*, *The Stone Face*, and *Return to Black America*, Smith left us with an extraordinary trilogy about the liberation, and the costs, of a black writer's exile in Europe. "The black person could live in greater peace with his environment in Copenhagen or Paris than in New York, not to speak of Birmingham or Jackson," he wrote:

> But he found it at times harder to live at peace with himself. The black man who established his home in Europe paid a heavy price. He paid it in a painful tearing of himself from his past.... He paid for it in guilt.... He paid for it, finally, in a sort of rootlessness: for, seriously, who were all these peculiar people speaking Dutch, Danish, Italian, German, Spanish, French?... What did they know about the black skin's long, bitter, and soon triumphant odyssey? The black man, no matter how long he lived in Europe, drifted through these societies as an eternal "foreigner" among eternal strangers.

Yet the stranger did not regret his journey. As he wrote in his unpublished memoir, "Through Dark Eyes," "this rootlessness has its inconveniences, but it has an advantage too: it gives a certain perspective." Smith's perspective—a radical humanism both passionate and wise, sensitive to difference but committed to universalism, anti-racist but averse to tribalism, disenchanted yet rebelliously hopeful—feels in dangerously short supply these days. It's time for his books to be restored to print, and for William Gardner Smith to be repatriated to the one country where he found a lasting home: the republic of letters.

—Adam Shatz

THE STONE FACE

To Edith

Whosoever hateth his brother is a murderer.

JOHN 3:15

I have been a stranger in a strange land.

EXODUS 2:22

PART ONE
The Fugitive

I

I

HE LEANED forward on the edge of his seat, his chin in his palms and his elbows on his knees, rocking imperceptibly to the movement of the train. It was evening, and in the fading light beyond the window the flat green-and-brown French farmland hurried by. He found his lips almost forming a prayer; not in words, not to a God, but in an emotion reaching out to the earth, the sky, to the world in general.

He was just under thirty and a Negro, and his name was Simeon Brown. He had only one eye; a black patch covered the socket of the other. He was tall and slender, with nervous, sensitive hands.

The others in the compartment chatted, but Simeon did not join in. His mind was beyond the train, outside, in the spring air, already in Paris.

A long journey, Simeon thought. America was behind him, his past was behind him, he was *safe*. Violence would not be necessary, murder would not be necessary. Paris. Peace.

2

He stood excited and shy in the long line waiting for a taxi. He felt the memory of his shyness in crowds and he automatically straightened his back, raised his head, stuck out his chin. Tall, wiry brown pirate with kinky hair and a black patch. As a child, before the protective patch-mask, Simeon had tried to overcome his shyness by a self-hypnotic chant: *You are a prince, you are a prince, you are a prince!* With his back straight and his eyes proud and level, the shyness would fade; he would walk like a prince, feel like a prince. Sometimes people said, "What a conceited boy, walks like he owns the world!" Razor words; but he had succeeded in concealing his shyness.

It was a warm evening in May 1960, and the streets near Gare Saint-Lazare were filled with people. Simeon was an amateur painter; he painted for his own amusement, and now he explored the passing faces to discover the characters they revealed. That Frenchwoman is dry, pinch-faced—unloved and therefore unloving, unhappy, destructive. This round flabby-faced man with startled eyes is lost—in a city, a world, a universe he does not understand. Torn by fears, petty ambitions. Trapped like most men in the hell of routine, never stopping to ask those maddening questions: Who are we? Where did we come from? Where are we going, and why? This young girl with swinging arms, darting eyes and health-flushed cheeks is *alive;* her face is a face of harmony. And these men, walking toward him in a group, with crinkly hair and skin which is not quite white but surely is not black? They had sullen, unhappy, angry eyes, eyes Simeon knew from the streets of Harlem. Baggy pants, worn shoes and shabby shirts. They glanced at Simeon unsmiling, and something strangely like recognition passed between him and them. Then they went on by him and disappeared.

3

Simeon found a room on the fourth floor of a small hotel on the rue de Tournon. He wanted to make no friends for a while. He explored the boulevards and small, twisting streets of the Latin Quarter, discovered the cafés where old men played cards all day. He admired the light in the spring sky, particularly at dusk, when the blue filtered through a silver haze.

One afternoon as Simeon sat at the Rhumerie Martiniquaise his eye was caught by the radiant face of a dark-haired young woman a few tables away from him.

For the first time since his arrival, Simeon felt lonely. It would be pleasant to talk to the woman, to try out his rusty college French. But his shyness returned at the thought of approaching an unfamiliar woman, white to boot.

Simeon stared at her. Suddenly she turned her head and her eyes met his. He felt hot and embarrassed. She looked at him with serene eyes and then, smiling faintly, turned the eyes away.

Shyness and desire warred in him. He hurried down his drink to give himself courage, then stood up abruptly and walked to her table. An absurd, frozen smile was on his lips.

"Pardon me," he said in halting French. "It's such a lovely day—I wondered if you would permit me to buy you a drink."

He was trembling idiotically. *You're a prince*, he told himself desperately, but he was too old; the fantasy no longer worked.

The smile flickered at the edges of the girl's mouth and eyes. Without looking up at him, she replied, "Thank you, no, Monsieur."

"I thought . . . I'm not trying to make advances. It's just such a lovely day . . ."

"No, Monsieur."

Simeon was mortified. He was certain that everyone on the terrace and on the street was staring at him. He was alone and naked on a stage, a blazing spotlight on him. The waiter appeared to be watching from the doorway of the café. Face burning like a torch, Simeon bowed stiffly and turned to walk back to his table. On the way, he tripped over the leg of a table and sent some glasses and bottles clattering to the floor. The young woman suppressed a laugh.

When he sat down again, Simeon cursed himself. Slowly, against his will, the old insidious thought came to him, the conditioned reflex. *Racism.* It was omnipresent. It was here in Paris, too. He turned the idea over in his mind, driving it into himself like a knife. There was an ache in the socket of the missing eye. He now detested the girl, with her mocking smile. He detested all of the people on the terrace who, he was still sure, were gloating over his humiliation.

Suddenly, the young woman's face lighted as she looked toward the street. She jumped up. A tall African, black as anthracite, walked smiling up to her. They embraced and kissed. The people on the terrace continued to talk, to sip their drinks, ignoring this scene as they had ignored the scene with Simeon.

The African and the young woman left the terrace arm in arm. As they passed Simeon, who could not help staring, the girl looked at him with a broader, mocking smile, and winked.

4

Simeon stood before the easel at the window of his room and dabbed with his paintbrush at a portrait he knew he would never finish. He had started the portrait over and over again. It was the massive head of a man sketched so harshly that it looked as though it had been carved out of stone; the jaw was clamped tight, the mouth was a compressed bitter line, the skin was deathly pale, the eyes were flat, fanatic, sadistic and cold. It was an inhuman face, the face of *un-man*, the face of discord, the face of destruction. As he stared at the portrait—the face of Chris, of Mike, of the sailor, he felt his old inescapable torment of emotions—horror, disgust, fear, hatred, and a desire to kill. It was this face that invited him to murder, that had almost sent him to the electric chair.

Let the peace of Europe be a medicine for me against this face, he thought.

He went downstairs. It was a warm, sunny afternoon. He passed a black woman who walked with easy gait holding hands with a Frenchman. Newspaper headlines shouted: MOSLEMS RIOT IN ALGIERS. FIFTY DEAD. A tramp lay in the gutter, his chin flecked with filth and stubby beard, his skin plowed like a field by drink. Death and misery walked the earth, but this Paris summer sun shone brightly. The tourists carrying cameras were gay. Simeon thought of the portrait and of America. "The child is father of the man."

A middle-aged man with swarthy skin and long crinkly hair pushed a cartload of fruit and vegetables. He looked like the group of men Simeon had seen outside the Gare Saint-Lazare when he arrived. Could these men be Algerians? Perspiring under the weight of the cart, the man looked at

Simeon with eyes which were neither friendly nor unfriendly, only curious. Simeon, for reasons he did not fully understand, felt a sudden flash of guilt.

As Simeon walked on he remembered how, at fourteen, he too had worked as delivery boy in a grocery store, pulling wagons of food through the streets of Philadelphia. He had worn sneakers with holes in them and old hand-me-down shirts and knickers torn at the knees. He remembered how groups of white people had stared at him—and how he had stared back, sullen, defiant, detesting their nice clothes and leisure and lazy, inquisitive eyes.

"Hi, daddy-o!"

The greeting, in a rumbling bass voice, was addressed to him by a black mountain of a man with a moon-shaped face sitting on the terrace of Le Tournon Café.

"Hi," Simeon answered.

"Take a seat, man. Relax the legs. Repose the buttocks. Enjoy the passing parade. Have a drink. You new over here, ain't you?"

Simeon sat at the table, facing the street, and stretched his long legs in front of him. "I've been here two weeks."

The mountain chuckled, a warm, friendly chuckle which boomed up from the cavernous stomach. "Can always tell you boys just come over from the States," he said. "You walk around lookin' all startled-like and freshly shaved in your well-pressed baggy-pants American clothes. My name's Babe Carter."

"Simeon Brown."

"Simeon. Funny name. But then our people got just about the funniest first names in creation. And then, how come we're all named Carter, Brown, Smith or Johnson? Some of them friggin' slave-owners musta really *messed up*! What you drinkin'? Beer? *Garçon! Une bière!* Glad to see you over here, Simeon. Like to see the boys get *out from under*. One less victim. Wish we could move the whole black population out of the States. How long you plannin' to stay in Europe?"

"A year at least."

Babe chuckled. "If you stay a year, you'll never go back."

"How long have you been here?"

"Ten years. And when I came over I just meant to stay two months."

Babe roared with laughter. His massive good humor was engaging, and intelligence shone through his tiny, sly, merry eyes. He was about forty, easily the biggest man Simeon had ever seen. He was well over six feet tall and gave the illusion of being just as big horizontally, yet he was not flabby. His gigantic arms and chest seemed on the verge of bursting through his thin white T-shirt. His coarse hair was clipped almost to the scalp, accentuating the roundness of his face.

"Ten years!" Babe roared triumphantly. "Seen 'em come and seen 'em go, as old Gibbon might say. Great town, if you don't weaken. If you can stand up under the drinkin' and the screwin' and the good food and wine." He sighed. "The things I've seen! Nice delicate little American fay chicks straight out of Barnard College who go down, down, once the brakes are off. Seen crackers become Negrophiles—at least, while they was *here*. Seen boys from rich famous families turn into bums because they couldn't keep away from women and wine. Seen bums turn into respectable people, too. Paris is a catalyst ... it'll break you or make you. Tell me, what brought *you* across the sea?"

Simeon looked at the black giant with a slight smile, then unexpectedly told the stranger what he had told no one else. "I left to prevent myself from killing a man."

Babe looked at him in astonishment. When he saw that Simeon was not joking, he rolled his eyes upward and raised his arms toward the sky. "Oops!" he said. "I ain't said a mumblin' word. *Them's* the kinda things I don't ask no questions about. Learned that lesson in the Harlem school of how to stay alive."

Simeon enjoyed watching Babe's mobile face. The man was obviously very much at home in Paris. Ten years. How long would he, Simeon, really stay? Would he go back to America afterward?

"Why did you come to France?" he asked Babe.

"Me? I came over to *get out from under*. Them people and their prejudice was on the verge of making me *thin*! So one day I just said, 'Okay, feet, let's get movin', this ain't no place for *me*.' You and me, we ain't the only ones. There's a new Lost Generation over here, lots of dark cats from the States who're here in Paris or in Copenhagen or Amsterdam or Rome or Munich or Barcelona, come over to get out from under that *pressure*, know what I mean? Ain't never going back, either. Some days when you walk down a street you see so many American Negroes you think you're back in Harlem."

Simeon drew on his cigarette and was startled by the sight of a tall long-legged girl with dark glasses, short-cropped black hair and an impudent walk who was crossing the street toward them. What jolted him was the luminosity of the handsome girl, who must have been in her early twenties; an aura of smoldering energy, a sort of electric field surrounded her, her face and bare legs *glowed* with health. She was very much aware of her beautiful body, exaggerating its movements like a child playing with a new toy. She seemed to dance as she moved toward the door of the café; then she saw Babe and smiled. She disappeared into the Tournon.

Simeon whistled softly. "Nice friends you've got Babe."

Babe chuckled. "You'll meet her. Name's Maria, she's Polish, come here on a trip from Poland to try to get into the movies and become another Brigitte Bardot. She damn sure is built like Brigitte. *Every*body's tryin' to make her, but no dice. She sits around with a bunch of Polish refugees inside the café. They're friends of her family, and they watch her like hawks."

They sat in silence then, drinking their beers and watching people stroll by. Simeon felt he had gone through his initiation now, this was *his* city. The old tension like poison had already begun to seep out of him, and he could feel himself growing strong and whole. He would become a new man. He wondered what that man would be.

Babe said, "What did you do in the States?"

"I was a newspaper reporter."

"There's a problem over here—making a living. You got any ideas?"

"I'd saved some money. Also, I'll be writing feature articles for a magazine called *He-Man*. You know, sex, sports, sex, auto racing, sex, guns and sex. The editor thinks I should find a lot of stuff to write for him in Gay Paree. . . . And you?"

"I got a little shop, a little bookstore. You'll see it later. Now, come on inside. Meet some of the people in the café."

5

Maria was just inside the door. She was playing the pinball machine with great intensity, her hips swiveling as she thumped the machine. She paid no attention to Simeon.

The café itself was a garish splash of green, yellow and red.

It was crowded, noisy, smoke-filled, with huge murals of the Luxembourg Gardens on the walls. Babe apparently knew everyone. They stopped before a group of tables where eight or nine young men and women sat, about half of them Americans.

"Meet Simeon, another refugee," Babe said.

Simeon shook hands all around. The people were dressed casually and most of them needed haircuts; their faces were pleasant, though the eyes of some were faintly red from lack of sleep or too much drink. All of them were white.

"Take a seat, join us," said a man named Lou. He had olive skin and intelligent eyes. He was playing chess with a girl.

"I'm from New York," he told Simeon. "I play jazz trumpet over here. Paris is a state of suspended animation. I really want to compose. I'll go back to New York in a year or so and settle down to serious work."

Another man Clyde, with a red face and dusty blond hair and mustache, was shouting at his wife, Jinx, in a heavy Southern accent. "Go ahead, keep it up, ruin yourself if you like. But don't go bringing no diseases home to me!"

Jinx, a New Yorker, had a harshly beautiful face with small, close, hysterical gray eyes and long hair she wore in a horse-tail that cracked like a whip about her shoulders.

"Darling, stop panicking in public. Besides, children are in the vicinity, my sweet."

Their six-year-old daughter, Jane, stared at them silently, then she left her parents and came to stand in front of Simeon, looking at him with cool sophistication.

"What happened to your eye?" she asked.

"It was a sacrifice."

"What's a sacrifice?"

"An offering. I gave it in exchange for something else."

"What did you get in exchange?"

"All the rest."

Simeon's eye was caught by Maria, the Polish girl, as she slapped her hip hard against the side of the pinball machine. She whirled, angry at the machine, and walked toward the rear of the café. She stopped when Babe called to her.

"Maria, come meet a newcomer—Simeon. He just got in town."

She stood in front of Simeon's table and Simeon, rising, held out his hand. She stared at him strangely, seeming undecided about something, and did not take the hand. The moment was long, Simeon feeling ridiculous with his hand in the air. Finally she flushed, as though in anger, shook his hand, and without a word turned abruptly and walked away.

Simeon was flabbergasted. Babe whistled softly, then grinned, his sly eyes narrowing. "Man, you been hiding things from ole Babe. What did *you* do to *her*?"

Simeon laughed, still dazed, and shook his head. "Damned if I know. Never saw her before in my life."

6

Maria was playing the pinball machine when Simeon went back to the Café Tournon the next afternoon. A group of Brazilians Simeon had met at the Alliance Française were playing guitars and singing in the rear of the café. Simeon stopped beside Maria and said "Bonjour."

She glanced up at him from behind the smoked glasses, then looked down at the machine again without saying anything. She wore a close-fitting black dress and he was fascinated by the curved long line between her hips and armpits. Her skin glowed like phosphorous.

"Why didn't you want to shake my hand yesterday?"

She shrugged in annoyance. Without looking up, she said, "It is because you are so conceited."

"Conceited?" His smile reflected amusement and surprise. "How can you say that? You don't even know me."

"I know you well enough." She spoke with a heavy Slavic accent, which made *well* sound like *waahhll*. She seemed embarrassed, as though she realized that what she was saying made sense to no one but herself. "I have seen you several times on the street. Walking with your head so high, like a king. Always I say to myself: 'Why does he walk like that, without even seeing other people, like he is better than everybody else?' And I think: 'Ha, here is one of those conceited men.'"

She blushed, glaring at the machine. Simeon's laugh irritated her. "I don't like conceited men," she said defiantly.

"I'm not conceited, I have a crick in my neck."

"Pardon? *Creek?* What is that?"

"A royal illness. Never mind. Will you have a drink with me?"

She hit the machine angrily with her open palm. "*Merde! I lose again! Always, always I lose. I don't know why I play. Yes, I take that drink."

They sat at a table in the rear. Simeon waved to Carlos and the other Brazilians.

"I take vodka," Maria said.

Simeon whistled. "In the afternoon!"

"I am *Pole!*" Maria said triumphantly. The waiter brought the drinks. "I do not stay long," Maria said. "Must go meet Paris mother."

"What does that mean, Paris mother?"

"Wife of Paris father. He is Polish refugee, friend of my family in Warsaw, takes care of me while I am here in Paris. I sit with him here sometimes; he is tall with very severe face. He gives me money to live here, and my uncle in Warsaw gives money to *his* relatives there."

"You are not a refugee?"

"No."

"You are going back?"

"I don't know yet. And you?"

"I don't know yet."

They were seated on opposite sides of the table, she on the cushioned bench, he on the chair with his back toward the door. She leaned on the table, inspecting him, and said, "What happen to your eye?"

He said, "It's better having only one. It concentrates, like a magnifying glass. The better to see beautiful Polish girls."

Her face lighted. "You think I am beautiful?"

She was pleased as a child. He said, "I think you're lovely."

Maria scowled. "You didn't act so! Walking with your head so high, seeing nobody on the street!"

She was infuriated by his roaring laughter. Simeon said, "How old are you?"

"I am twenty-four. Why?"

"In many ways, you make me think of a child."

"Is good to be a child." Simeon thought he heard a hint of defiance in her voice.

Simeon wanted to see her eyes. "Why do you hide your eyes behind dark glasses?"

She shrugged, looking beyond him to the door. "I must. Eyes weak. I am becoming blind."

She said it so simply, so casually, that Simeon was not sure he had heard her correctly.

"Blind?"

She looked at him again, vaguely annoyed. It was evidently something she did not want to think about. "It's a long story. Anyway, it is not certain. The doctors in Poland could do nothing, but they said maybe specialists in France could save my eyes. I am having treatments. In some months I will have an operation. Maybe they can be saved. Nobody knows."

He was moved. She saw his face and laughed. "Don't look like it's a funeral already. Is not sure. Besides, what counts is the present. I want to live in present. You understand me? I want to live."

"What do you mean by *live*?"

"Enjoy self. Not worry about things. Do all things I always want to do—laugh, sing, dance, see bright lights. Froth, I want *froth* of life for once, you understand me? Maybe that sounds bad. Is not bad."

She sipped her vodka and thought for a moment, frowning. "I tell you something. People like me, who are young in Poland, we have not had much *froth*. First the war, and I cannot describe to you that war, a horrible war, barbarous war. War of annihilation, you understand? My mother and father dead, friends dead, everything in ruins. And after war it is necessary to build everything from nothing. We are poor, everything is cold and gray. Government says, 'We must sacrifice now, build for future.' I do not criticize the government, I do not make politics, you understand? But we, young ones, we tired of sacrifice. Is weakness, maybe. But the young ones get tired, they want play a little, want have their childhood. Life cannot always be gray, one must have colors sometime."

She stopped, caught her breath: "So doctors tell me, 'You are becoming blind, you be blind maybe in two-three years.'

I say, 'Yes, all right, I be blind, but first I see. First, I see colors in life, something besides gray.' So I come to Paris. I want play like child, play games like child for while. Maybe become actress, so I go to drama school. Visit other countries. See bright lights, dance, sing, laugh. Even play pinball machine, you see. We had no such *froth* as pinball machine when I was child."

Looking at her now, Simeon saw for the first time something more than a pretty empty-headed doll. He was astonished by the extraordinary contrast between what she seemed externally and what she felt and had lived. This child-role was a mask; there were nightmares inside her head. He thought of his own former nightmares, of the portrait of the face in his room. For years that face had been at the center of all his dreams. Sometimes the face simply floated in the air. Sometimes it perched itself on the bodies of people Simeon knew: neighbors, schoolteachers, and even on occasion his brothers or father. Walking in a dream field on a pleasant day, he would see the face pop up from behind a stone or leer through the branches of a tree. Sometimes it shone burning in the sky, a horrifying sun.

Maria said, "You are American, no?"

"Yes."

"Lots of bright lights there, far from the grayness. Lots of comfort, lots of big houses and big cars, yes?"

"Yes."

"Then why did you leave?"

"To escape the grayness."

"You joke."

"No."

II

I

WHEN SIMEON had been a boy in Philadelphia, on Tenth Street just off South, where children yelled as they ran in oversize knickers and garbage rotted on the street, "The Chase" had been the game which had excited him most.

The Chase: a game, a sport, an entertainment for simmering summer evenings when the sun leaned red over the rooftops and boredom threatened with approaching night. A ball, the key to the game, was tossed lazily back and forth in the street among the sweating boys. Old folks sat on the scrubbed marble steps, gossiping and fanning away mosquitoes and flies. Rattletrap street cars went noisily by. Radios shrieked baseball results, the Jack Benny Show, The March of Time, jazz, or, on Sundays, Elder Johnson's gospel choir. On the sidewalks, languid, watching the boys, stood the girls.

Back and forth, back and forth went the ball, as the stifling air heated more than skin. Old folks talked about the Race Problem, about Our Folks and Them Folks. Dim, still-alive memory of the other, physical, chains. The girls stirred, watching the boys. The girls exchanged nervous glances, words, smiles. The boys saw the smiles and the restlessness. The girls whispered, giggled; the boys saw them whisper, heard them giggle; and then suddenly it would begin, the gradual thickening of tension, the trembling perspiration of the hands, the accelerated heartbeats and the hot obstruction of throats. No one said anything. Outwardly, nothing changed. But the electricity was there in the humid summer air, and all of them knew that The Chase was about to begin.

The tossed ball would seem to float in the air. A girl would dart from the pavement into the street, leap with hand upstretched into the air and snatch the ball in flight. Laughing, she would then stand between the two groups of boys, holding the ball in her hand, stretching the hand toward them teasingly. "Come get it, come get it." Meanwhile, the other girls would have raced up to the end of the street, far beyond the boys. Gristle or Joe or Snakes would say: "Okay, okay, Sarah, give us the ball." Sarah would laugh. "Come take it from me, if you're big enough!"

The boys would look at each other, shrug, grin and begin closing in on the girl. She would hold the ball temptingly at arm's length. They would come closer, closer, and when they were very near Sarah would howl with glee and hurl the ball with all her strength up the street, to the other girls. Laughing in triumph, then, Sarah would dash through the ranks of the boys and run to join the other girls.

"If you want the ball, come git it!" cried the girls.

The boys would look at one another. "Let's go git 'em," one of them would say.

In no particular hurry, at an easy trot, the boys would start up the street toward the girls. Shrieking with delight and fear, the girls kicked up their heels and ran around the corner, onto South Street. The Chase was on.

How far did they run? For miles it had always seemed to Simeon. Around corners, across squares, through alleys, up and down big streets and small. Down the stairs of subway stations and up into the dusk again. They ran until they could no longer breathe, until their muscles ached and the sweat-chilled shirts clung to their bodies; and still they ran, until their legs groaned and their heads swam, ran until the "breakthrough" came, until they got their second wind and could breathe again. White folks turned and stared at them, and shook their heads. Motorists cursed, applying shrieking brakes. Policemen glared suspiciously: niggers running—they must of stolen something!

From time to time the girls, when they could really bear to run no longer, slowed down to a walk. So did the boys. Their aim, now, was not so much to catch the girls as to keep them in sight, keep the distance between them constant. The girls giggled and whispered again in excited complicity, glancing nervously behind them to make certain the boys were not sneaking closer. Boy to boy: "That Reety sure is got some *fine* legs!" Boy to boy: "Look at Sarah's nice big jelly-roll ass!"

In this way they crossed the city, the Negro neighborhoods and the white, passed Italians, Poles, Irish, Jews, Anglo-Saxons, running the gamut of races, nationalities and classes. Sweat poured from their young bodies. Dirty old shirts hanging out of dirty old pants. Their eyes glistened and their bellies were furnaces.

They would finally reach the outskirts of the city, the endless wasteland of vacant lots covered with twisted grass and littered with stones, cans, bottles, papers and other refuse. Here, on the brink, the girls hesitated, dizzy and terrified; wanting to shout for help, to be safe at home, at mother's knee. They turned terrorstricken eyes on the approaching boys, whose frozen smiles belied their trembling legs, the unbearable drumming of their hearts. The boys came on relentlessly.

Turning, in a dream, the girls dashed onto the grass, running and screaming, running as though for dear life now, falling, getting up, running again. The lumbering bull-boys ran, too—no longer talking and joking, no longer trying merely to keep the girls in sight, but running in earnest, running to trap and hold and take. In the fast-fading dusk, the distance between the two groups narrowed swiftly. The girls cried for help with all their might, but there was no one to hear; their screams rolled out across the wasteland of lots and up to the darkening sky. The foremost boy leaped and tackled the nearest girl, bringing her roughly to the ground. One by one each of the girls felt hungry hands seize her and hold her and throw her to the grass. There were not enough girls for all the boys. No matter: two boys could take one girl

What always followed, though not precisely rape, had always seemed like rape to Simeon. The girls kicked and clawed and punched and bit. The boys held them fast, forcing their dresses up and their drawers down. Exhausted, overpowered, the girls were taken one by one. Nightfall, and strange sounds in the silence of the twisted grass. Sweat mingling with sweat. Eventually it was over. All of them, boys and girls, lay on their backs among the cans and stones, smoking cigarettes and staring dazedly at the star-filled sky. How long did they lie there, silent and alive? For half an hour, an hour perhaps. Then, slowly, the girls stood up, brushed their skirts, looking at each other sheepishly, and walked off in a group for the long journey home. Shortly afterward, the boys stood up and followed them.

2

Child with marveling eyes, leaning on the bedroom window, looking at the night sky, wondering: *Where does space end? It never ends. But that's impossible! When did time begin? It never began and will never end. But that's impossible! Where did people come from? Why?*

Sensitivity was a curse, that marked the world of Simeon's childhood. It was a violent world.

The big family jammed into a five-room house. Grandpa, Grandma, Mom, Pop, aunts, uncles and five sisters and brothers. A family of laborers and domestic servants. There was little air in that house, and not much affection. Destiny was the rent man, the insurance man, the breadman, the milkman, the refrigerator man, the furniture man, the grocer. Simeon was a grocery delivery boy and general helper after school, at three dollars and fifty cents per week. It was fun if you turned it into a game: the deliveries were secret missions, the tin cans were soldiers which he lined in battle order on the shelves. On Saturdays he loved to browse among the books at the public library or sometimes even listen to records in the music room of the Logan Square Library.

The six children slept in two beds in one room. There were two girls and four boys, so Simeon, the youngest, was put in the bed with the girls. Sometimes at night his nervous hands explored his older sister's body. She never moved, but he always thought she was only pretending to be asleep. Each child slept in his underwear, and they woke up two or three times every night to brush the bedbugs from the sheets.

On winter mornings the boys got up early to clean and light the kitchen stove and build up the fire in the cellar furnace. They boiled salted water on the kitchen stove and added flakes of oatmeal to make their breakfast before going to school. Winter was the time of peril. Their bedrooms were heated by rickety kerosene stoves on flimsy legs; the stoves blazed red at night; four times in Simeon's childhood the stoves had been knocked over, four times the flaming kerosene had hissed along the floor and caught at the furnishings and the wall. It was a miracle that none of them had ever been seriously hurt. Rats lived in the cellar, giant rats which entered from the broken sewers. Sometimes they invaded the house itself, and rat traps and poison were everywhere. When they had been very young, a rat had scrambled into the bed and chewed at the hand of Simeon's youngest sister. It was strange that she did not wake up.

Violence was in the streets and in the schools. Individual fights, gang wars, race wars. Inexplicable violence, purposeless violence. Before this Simeon recoiled.

"C'mon! C'mon! Put up your fists!"

"Hey, Simeon, put on a suit and meet all the boys on the corner tonight, there's gonna be a dance."

He did not want to go. There was always trouble at the dances. Of course he could not let the others think he was afraid; he had to go.

But he asked, trying to sound casual: "You think the Northsiders will try to break in?"

"Who cares? Whatsamatter, you scared?"

"Who, me? Scared? Hell, no!"

"We'll beat the livin' shit outta them if they show up."

And of course they showed up. There was a riot, knives were drawn and people injured and even killed in a bedlam of insane curses and screams. Simeon was knocked flat on his back by a chair, trampled by fleeing feet as the police vans arrived. He did not know how he managed to get home.

His aunt bathed the head wound. He lay in the dark room unable to sleep, and late at night got out of bed and went to stand at the window. There was peace up there, in that sky of stars. What he wanted was to attain that peace. But that was impossible. The world was here, and it was violent and brutal. Wasps killed spiders and spiders killed flies. That was the Law. The world made sensitivity a curse; one had to live within the Law.

He prayed softly to the sky: "Make me strong, make me a man. Make me respected by the others, make me brave and tough. I don't want to be soft; I want to be strong. I'll make a sacrifice, take a sacrifice in exchange. I'd give anything, make any sacrifice, to be strong and respected, to be a man."

The next day, his grandmother said: "Go around on Reed Street to the Italian store and get me some spaghetti sauce."

Simeon was frightened. The Poles and Italians lived in that neighborhood, and they were at war with the Negroes.

"What you waiting for, Simeon? You hear me?"

He was ashamed. "It's them Poles, Grandma. They having a war with the colored boys."

"You ain't scared of no white boys, is you?"

"No'm."

"Ain't no grandson of mine supposed to be scared of no white boys. You go buy me that sauce."

He made his way toward Reed Street as slowly as possible. He paused at every store window, kicked every stone he saw. But he knew he was simply delaying his arrival; he knew he was afraid, and he was furious with himself. *"Ain't no grandson of mine supposed to be scared...."* What sacrifice could he make to acquire toughness? "I'll give a—a toe," he suggested tentatively, looking up at the sky. The sky gave no indication that it accepted the bargain, and he had a suspicion that a toe would not be enough. Besides, it would hurt, cutting off a toe. He grimaced.

Now he was on Reed Street and up ahead, on a corner, he saw a group of boys, most of them Poles. With them was a tall kid named Chris, leader of the gang and the toughest boy in their neighborhood. He had a solid reputation for hating Negroes. Simeon swallowed hard. He wanted to cross to the other side of the street, but something inside him, some deep core of pride, made him stay on the pavement. The group appeared not to notice him and Simeon continued cautiously on his way, walking as close to the curb as possible.

"Hey, *nigger*!"

He wanted to run but his muscles froze.

"C'mere, nigger."

He felt that a brave person should say something defiant, throw the word *nigger* back into their faces. But his tongue was paralysed.

His sense of time was distorted: everything was in slow motion. The boys stood around him, who now saw them through a blur, the leader, Chris, standing in front of Simeon, studying him with a faint cold smile. Chris toyed with a jagged switchblade knife. Everything was a blur, and then suddenly Chris' face came into frightening sharpness. He had an inhumanly cold face with dull, sadistic eyes, a thin mouth, tightly clamped jaw and deathly pale skin. Chris' face was utterly without feeling; it betrayed a soul of stone. Chris suddenly became aware that Simeon was staring at his face, and his sheet-white skin reddened.

"Whatchu lookin at, nigger?"

Simeon said nothing.

"Nigger don't like to talk. Hold him." The boys held Simeon, twisting his arms behind him.

Chris said, "Nigger don't like my face. Tell me it's a pretty face, nigger. Tell me it's a prettier face than your mammy's got."

Simeon continued to stare, hypnotized by the glazed blue eyes of his tormentor. For the instant he was less frightened by the danger than by the coldness of the eyes, the iron jaw. *The man who had this face felt no human emotion, no compassion, no generosity, no wonder, no love!* The face was that of *hatred:* hatred and denial—of everything, of life itself. This was the terrible face of anti-man, of discord, of disharmony with the universe. What horrors could have turned a human being into this?

Chris placed the razor-edged knife at Simeon's throat and said with sudden fury: *"Answer* me, nigger, or I'll *blind* you!"

Terror washed over him. Simeon almost fainted. He forced his mouth open, forced out the word: "Yes."

The flat eyes burned into his. "Yes *what*?" All else shimmered, was indistinct; there was only this face in the universe, shining with the joy of destruction.

"Yes, it's a pretty face."

"Prettier than your mammy's!"

"Yes."

"Say it!"

"Prettier than my mother's."

"Mammy's, nigger!"

"Prettier… than my mammy's."

"Prettier than your rotten, no good, cock-suckin' mammy's. *Say it!*"

The face shone. It grew brighter, a satanic star, burning with hatred and evil. Simeon shut his eyes against it. His legs gave way but the boys held him up. The world reeled.

"*Say it!*"

He opened his mouth, but no words would come out. He could hardly breathe. He opened his eyes and looked pleadingly at the stone face.

"Say it, nigger, I'm telling you one more time."

Simeon closed his eyes again and fell into a kind of stupor. Dear God, Dear God, Dear God, he cried inside himself. But the prayer was interrupted by a shrieking flash of brilliant color, followed instantly by a blazing pain. He could not hear himself screaming. "Jesus, you blinded him!" a boy yelled. Simeon screamed at the peak of his voice, falling to the pavement, darkness closing in on him, his hands clutched to the place where he had once had an eye.

3

Black patch. "Only temporary," the doctor said to his mother. "Later you can buy a glass eye to put in the socket."

But Simeon had never wanted the glass eye.

Out of the hospital, walking up Tenth Street: "Damn! Look at Simeon!"

"Hey! You look like somebody in a movie, Simeon!"

"You look like a war lord!"

"You look like a pirate!"

War lord? Pirate? Simeon stared at himself in the mirror with satisfaction.

The girls were fascinated. "Simeon, you look ... tough. You look ... mysterious, romantic."

Tough? Mysterious? Romantic? Simeon faced the mirror and barked commands to invisible followers: "Captain, place your men on that hill. You, Colonel, protect the rear. I'll lead the main attack." He injected courage into faltering troops: "Forward! Let's show them how to die like men!" His mind took him to distant countries where he entered ballrooms and exotic restaurants. Everyone was in awe of the Man of Mystery!

"This eye," Simeon told the boys of the neighborhood, "is a gift to the gods. I gave them the eye; they give me other things."

The boys looked at him sceptically. "Such as?"

"Strength, courage, bravery—"

"Hah!"

One of the boys was toying with a penknife. For a terrifying instant Simeon saw the face of Chris before him. He said, "Lend me the knife."

Holding the knife like a dagger in his right hand, Simeon turned up the palm of his left. Everyone watched in amazement as he raised the knife high over the open palm. "What in hell you gonna do?" He inhaled deeply, thought of Chris and brought the knife down hard into his palm. The boys gasped; the girls squealed. The knife trembled in the palm. He had not flinched. For a moment he let the group stare at the upright knife, then pulled it brutally out of his hand.

"Goddam!" a boy whispered admiringly.

The girls rushed toward him. "Simeon, you're *crazy!*" He let himself be led away, allowed his hand, now covered with blood, to be washed, spread with iodine and bandaged. "Goddam! Goddam!" the boys kept repeating.

Simeon smiled. He was a man.

III

I

ONE DAY Simeon walked over to Babe's English-language bookshop, a small store on the rue Monsieur le Prince. The window was well decorated, and the store had the most recent American and English books, in addition to Henry Miller and other books still banned in the United States. A young Frenchwoman behind the counter showed Simeon the stairs leading to Babe's apartment on the second floor. Babe's huge frame filled the entire doorway. "Come on in, man, we're just opening up a bottle of *vin rouge*."

He introduced Simeon to five other Negroes in the big, comfortable living room: two women jazz singers, Gertie and Mathilda, and three men, Doug, Harold and Benson. "Harold's one of the best classical composers around," Babe said, "and Benson is a novelist."

"*Used* to be a novelist," Benson said. He looked about forty-five, a handsome man with graying temples and an ironic expression in his pale brown eyes.

"James Benson?" Simeon said. "I've read some of your books. Very strong, very bitter."

There was something said in Benson's eyes, his face and movements gave an impression of weariness. He drank some of the red wine. "Ain't gonna be no more books. I ain't got nothing more to say to them people. Said all I got to say. I'm a *journalist*, now. Write crap from Paris for the *Black Dispatch*. Tole Babe to stop that novelist crap."

"When was it you wrote your last book?"

"Ten years ago. Ain't got nothing more to say to them people."

Babe grinned, handing Simeon a glass of wine. "See that character over there—that mouselike gloomy character in the corner? He's a *government man!*"

Doug, who was somewhat younger than Simeon, *did* look like a mouse. His bony face moved forward toward a point; he had enormous, indignant eyes and huge ears.

He gave Babe a pained and furious look. "I keep tellin' you, you oughtn't say things like that to people. They might take you seriously." He spoke with a heavy Southern drawl.

"I *am* serious. You work for the government or not?"

"I'm a minor clerk in the Embassy. That ain't the same thing."

"Who pays you?"

Doug frowned and looked at the floor. "You know who pays me." Simeon smiled. Doug was a perfect straight man.

"There you go. So you a *government* man. A government *agent*."

Benson laughed a wicked laugh, looking at Doug's downcast face. Gertie, who was almost as big as Babe, winked and said soothingly, "That's all right, Doug, don't let 'em get you down, hear? Stick up for your rights; *I'm* on your side."

Simeon drank from the glass. It was pleasant to be in this apartment with other American Negroes. After a while he would look for a place and move out of that hotel room. He had time. He stood at the window and on the street below saw an African walking slowly with his arm around a girl. Benson came over and stood beside him.

"Babe tells me you're a newsman, too."

"Writing stupid stuff for a stupid magazine."

"We write crap together, then."

"The books you wrote weren't crap."

"That was when I was young and indignant. You have to believe in something to be indignant."

"You stopped writing books when you left the States?"

"That's right."

"If you'd stayed there, do you think you'd have continued writing?"

"Maybe."

"And you still don't want to go back?"

Benson chuckled. "Ole Beethoven. He was deaf, you know. Some people say he might not have written all that great music if he hadn't been deaf." After a pause, Benson said, "Me, I want to keep my hearing."

2

The following Saturday Babe called for Simeon at his hotel. They were to meet two Swedish girls for dinner. Babe had to lower his head to get through the doorway; his mountainous figure seemed to fill the room. Babe looked at Simeon's paintings

Simeon said, "I liked Benson. I read a novel of his when I was a kid, a brilliant book. It's a damned shame he's stopped writing."

"Yeah. He don't like to talk about it much. He says he just suddenly felt like *silence*. He's a strange cat, a sort of hermit. Disappears into his apartment with whatever girl he happens to be living with. He really hates all the girls he lives with, even while he's with them, because they're white. A bitter man who don't believe in much any more, not even in himself. He's one of the boys, though."

Simeon noticed that at times Babe completely dropped his slurring Negro drawl. He "wore" the drawl whenever he wanted to. He now stared at the canvas on the easel: the inhuman face Simeon had once again begun to paint. The cold eyes shone from the canvas with quiet cruelty.

"What is *that?*"

"It's the man I told you about. The man I almost killed."

"He doesn't look real. It look like it was carved out of rock . . . or out of wax. Who is he?"

"That's a long, long story, Babe."

Babe looked at Simeon with mock saucers of eyes and slipped back into the Negro drawl. "Man, you is one of them *excitable* people! One of them gun-tottin', knife-wieldin', bottle-throwin' kind! Gotta watch my step with you!"

They took a taxi to the Champs-Élysées, where they were to meet the Swedish girls. Babe leaned back comfortably, puffing on his pipe, his eyes narrowed in thought. More went on in that head than one might gather from the easy banter, Simeon thought. Simeon made himself as comfortable as possible in what Babe had left him of the seat, and watched the people, the cafés, the trees and the bridges of the Seine go by. He was amazed to find himself relaxed and calm. Sometimes in Paris he dreamed that he was back in Philadelphia, unable to escape. Slowly, as consciousness came, the terror faded. Yes, it was all right; he was in Paris.

But the old reflexes died hard. He felt a vague unease, a readiness for battle as they left the taxi and walked to the café where the girls waited for them. Babe kissed Marika on the cheek; Simeon shook Ingrid's hand. They had met the girls the day before—pretty, empty-headed but gay.

They ate at Les Îles, a cozy restaurant on the rue Marbeuf, off the Champs-Élysées. Chickens turned on spits, people talked gaily. The waiters were polite. Simeon remembered that when you went into the fashionable restaurants of Philadelphia with a black skin, waiters would step forward quickly to say: "Sorry, there are no tables."

After dinner Babe took them to a key club on the Left Bank. It was a small club dimly lighted by candles, where one could dance to Latin American and jazz records. As they came in, a French girl in a tight-fitting dress was going through the gyrations of the Twist.

"Nothing like this in Stockholm," Ingrid said, frowning. "The men are dull—and they're not interested in girls. It's the dullest place in the world."

"The men are too blond," Marika said.

Babe laughed. "You're pretty blond yourself."

"With women it's *different*."

Ingrid's body pressed close to Simeon as they danced to the slow blues. She had a cold, depersonalized, lovely face; still, it was pleasant dancing with a woman again. Simeon talked politely and she nodded and smiled, a good listener.

They returned to the table. The manager of the club came over and talked to Babe, whom everybody in Paris seemed to know. Then the door to the club opened and four men walked in, all Americans. Their drunken raucous laughter and loud voices disturbed the peaceful atmosphere of the room. The manager seated them at a table adjacent to Simeon's and one of them called imperiously for a waiter: "Champagne. Champagne for me and my friends. We got plenty of money, bring on the champagne."

They were no doubt businessmen on vacation, doing Paris by night. Simeon felt less American than ever before. Were Negroes such a separate nation within that nation which was America? The mood in the club was shattered now for Simeon; his mind became fixed on the four men at his elbow, engaged in the desperate American occupation of trying to enjoy themselves. They drank, shouted, told unfunny jokes, laughed the tense laughs of nervous compulsion. Then their eyes fell on Simeon and Babe and the Swedish girls.

The four men grinned. "Hey, you boys from the States?"

There was no reply.

"What's the matter? I'm just being friendly. Good to meet other Americans over here, that's all. Get tired of these god-dam frogs."

Babe said, "Man, we ain't no boys. I'm old enough to be your mother's husband."

The man laughed nervously. "Where you from in the States? I'm from Utah, myself; me and my friends here we're over on a short trip but we can't wait to get back. But I bet you boys like it over here, all right. Never had it so good, huh, all these blondes and things. *Hah, hah, hah.*"

His loud voice filled the room, and the other people in the club were silent. Then Simeon said, "That's right, never had it so good being away from *you*."

"What'd I do? How come you people are so touchy all the time?"

One of his friends said, "Skip it, Jim. Come on, drink your champagne. Them boys' bigger'n their britches over here where the frogs let 'em run around loose." He pointed a finger at Simeon. "I got one bit of advice for you, boy. Stay over here. You done got sassy since you come over here, but we'll sure as hell change that if you come back home!"

The waiter and the manager had been watching the scene from a distance, and now, as Simeon and Babe rose from their table and moved toward the four men, the manager stepped forward.

"I'm sorry," he said to the white men. "I have to ask you to leave." They were astonished. One man said, "What's this? You crazy or something? You gonna throw out white men for niggers?"

The manager said in perfect English, "Please leave or I'll call the police. There are certain things you have to leave behind when you come to France. At least when you come to my club."

"We was just saying to them boys——"

The manager nodded to several waiters, who started toward the Americans. The man named Jim said, "Okay, okay. Let's go, fellas." He looked at the manager and shook his head. "You must be out of your mind, mister." At the door, one man turned and shouted to Simeon and Babe: "Remember what I told you, boys. You better stay over here with these nigger-lovers, 'cause you'd have a lot of painful lessons to learn again in the States."

The door closed. People in the club looked at Simeon and Babe with smiles of relief. The manager shook his head. "Sorry, Babe. Your compatriots—they have disagreeable reflexes sometimes."

Babe chuckled. "Don't I know it. Them people got a long way to go, a lot to learn."

"Have a drink," the manager said. He smiled. "How about some champagne? *Their* champagne."

Marika said, "What I can't understand is what was it all about? What happened?"

"It's a long story, Baby," Babe said. "I don't think they really meant to be that way. They just open their mouths and they can't help putting their feet in them."

It was late when they left the club. Babe laughed as they walked down the street. "Maybe they didn't mean no harm, them paddies, but it sure feels good sometimes to have the shoe on the other foot."

"Yes."

At the corner, they saw a policeman clubbing a man. Although he had fallen to the pavement, the policeman kept on swinging his long white nightstick down on the man, who was trying in vain to protect his head from the blows with his arms. The man was screaming in a language Simeon could not understand. Simeon watched the beating until the patrol wagon pulled up and two policemen tossed the beaten man into the back and drove off.

"What was *that*?" Simeon asked.

Babe said, "The man was probably an Arab."

"An Arab?"

"Yeah. There's a war on in Algeria, remember?"

"Oh. Yes."

3

"Hey, Joe Louis, come here."

It was a spring evening in Philadelphia. Simeon had been moving ahead in the world then, had been to Penn State on a scholarship, studied journalism, and become the first Negro reporter in town on a "white" newspaper. That evening, he had visited white friends, former schoolmates at college, in a pleasant residential neighborhood. Afterward, he went to the bus stop, where a white couple were already waiting. A police patrol car passed, halted, backed up and shone its searchlight on him. A policeman leaned out of the window and beckoned to him.

Simeon did not move; he pretended not to see the cop. He knew why they were calling: a Negro was "out of place" in a white neighborhood. Rage, always just below the surface, began to boil up in him. He knew what to expect.

"Hey, Joe Louis, come here."

He did not move. From the corner of his eye, he saw that there were two policemen in the car. The white couple looked at him apprehensively, as though he were a dangerous criminal wanted by the police. One of the cops cursed and got out of the automobile and strode over to him.

"Didn't you hear me call you?"

"My name's not Joe Louis."

"Oh, one of them *bad* ones! What're you doin' in this neighborhood this time of night, boy?"

"I'm not a boy. I'm as old as you are."

"You been up to some mischief? You been stealing something, boy?"

His rage boiled over. "I been looking for your sister!"

The cop's face went white, his open right hand exploded against Simeon's cheek. Simeon did not even have time to think: his fist leaped up from his side and crashed against the policeman's chin. The cop went sprawling; there was a split second of dazed amazement, then: "Why you black mother——," and he reached for his pistol. The second policeman jumped from the car. "No, Mike, not that!" he shouted. He waved his own pistol at Simeon with a smile. "Okay, Joe Louis, get in the car."

They drove off. Simeon sat in the back, saying nothing. Mike whistled. "Nice punch you got there, Joe Louis. One thing I like, it's a spirited nigger. How about that, Jeff?" "Yeah," the other cop said, "We love spirited niggers."

They took him to the police station. Cops lolled about everywhere, sitting on the edges of tables or on chairs, some playing cards. They were relaxed, smoking, telling dirty jokes, their coats off and their shirtsleeves rolled up. Mike shoved Simeon toward the sergeant's desk. "Resisting arrest, assaulting an officer, Sarge." The sergeant booked him. Mike said, "Before you stow him away, we'd like to have a little private conversation with him." "Sure," the sergeant said, and got up. "I'm going out to buy some cigarettes. Be back in an hour or so," he announced. Mike looked at Simeon and grinned. "He's a great guy, the Sarge. Understands things."

Mike and Jeff led Simeon into a back room. Some of the lolling policemen who were not playing cards said "What's up?"

"This guy's a boxer," Jeff said. "Joe Louis. Knocked Mike out in one round."

The cops whistled softly and came to watch. Mike smiled, taking off his jacket. "I always did have a glass jaw if you caught me right. Joe Louis there caught me right, didn't you, boy?" He chuckled, shaking his head. "Okay, Joe Louis, take off your clothes."

Simeon did not move. He was not going to make things easier for them. He was scared; he hated himself for being scared.

Mike moved forward and hit him in the face with his fist.

Simeon crumbled under the blow. "Not so tough here are you, Joe Louis!" A policeman snorted in disgust. "Fell with the first punch. Niggers are yellow!" Jeff said, "Well, now, you gotta be fair. Mike fell with the first punch, too." Mike, Jeff and another cop pulled Simeon to his feet and began beating him methodically. He tried to protect the socket of his eye with his hands, but two other policemen came and pinioned his arms behind him. Mike pounded his stomach and groin; Simeon's face twisted, and he fainted.

When he came to, he was naked on the wooden floor. Mike and Jeff were holding lengths of rubber hose, while the other cops sat on a table smoking and watching him.

Mike bent over him and smiled. "Feel better, Joe Louis?"

His entire body ached, and he could hardly see out of his one eye.

Mike said, "Joe Louis, I'm gonna tell you why I like spirited niggers. It's because it's so much fun putting them back in their place. Know what I mean? This is a white man's country, boy; we don't want your black ass here stinking up the place nohow, but long as you're here you're damn sure gonna stay in your place. Now, you know who I am? I'm your tutor. I'm the special archangel sent specially to look after you, keep you out of mischief and stuff. And I'm a responsible sort of man, I'm gonna fill that role. I got your address. I'll drop in to see you from time to time. I'm gonna personally keep my eye on you. And any time you act up, I'll bring you in for treatment again. Personally. A sort of marriage, you know, between me and you."

Mike raised the hose and it fell with unbelievable weight across Simeon's abdomen. He doubled up with a stifled cry. The hose fell again and again. Mike kept talking softly, soothingly, in whispered joy, and suddenly, seeing in a flash the hard mouth and sadistic eyes Simeon thought: *It's the same face!* The face of Chris! The illusion lasted an instant only. A blow of the hose snapped him like a switchblade. The hose chopped at the base of his neck. Hoses fell from everywhere, while the distant, toneless, strangely soothing voice of Mike went on: "You see, boy, hoses don't leave no marks. I don't mean you no harm. I want to keep you out of trouble. I'm your guardian angel; we're married from now on, you and me." And then the world again became black.

Guardian Angel Mike. Simeon bought a pistol from a friend who had been in the Army. But Mike did not come to his house. He never saw Mike again.

IV

I

THE CAVALCADE of ten cars was pulling into a clearing in the forest south of Paris. Carlos, one of Babe's Brazilian friends, had suggested the trip, saying that they should take wine, beer and food to a spot in the Chevreuse Valley from which they could overlook the entire forest. "We can roast lamb over an open fire and listen to guitars until morning!" Carlos' idea had enchanted them and they left Paris in great excitement. Most of the Americans from the Tournon crowd had come, as well as the Brazilians and others from the quarter. There were about forty people in all, who now piled out of the cars and began climbing the hill.

Simeon held Maria's hand and carried a case of wine on his shoulder. Stones slid beneath their feet. Below them Babe huffed and puffed, shoving his immense body up the hill. They finally reached the small plateau at the top, where those who had already arrived were searching for firewood. Maria sank onto a blanket and Simeon went off to look for wood. Eventually Babe reached the top, wheezing like an engine, the Swedish girl Marika beside him. Babe collapsed onto a blanket. "It ain't right, it ain't right," he said. "Some people got so much more weight to carry around than others. It ain't right."

Simeon felt elated by the air and the view. Maria did not move, but lay on her back, staring in a melancholy and inscrutable way at the sky. Every time he had looked at her, since their first meeting, intense physical desire had overwhelmed him. It was not just because of her body—he had seen other lovely bodies—but because of a turbulent, somber passion he felt beneath her usual silence. This woman was a sleeping volcano, radically different from other women he had known. Suddenly, without giving his shyness time to assert itself, Simeon bent down and kissed her on the cheek. She did not move, but lay on her back, staring in a melancholy and inscrutable way at the sky.

Soon two fires were blazing in the clearing, the lambs turning over them slowly on spits. They sat in a huge circle around the fires. The sun had gone completely now, and the night breeze was cool and fresh. Below stretched the forest and in the distance they could see the highway with the headlights of cars, and beyond that, on the horizon, the lights of Paris. Simeon lay on his back, Maria beside him. The Brazilians passed a bottle of Beaujolais to each person shouting, "First course."

They all began to drink the wine and Babe, the best storyteller Simeon had ever heard, started telling jokes. Harold, the composer Simeon had met at Babe's bookshop, was staring wistfully into the fire.

"What are you thinking, Harold?" Simeon asked.

There was a frown on Harold's face; he turned his soft, liquid-brown eyes on Simeon and said, "I'm thinking about a piano." He had a velvet voice with a Midwestern twang. "Look, it's hard enough to find an apartment in Paris, right? But whenever I manage to find one I'm happy and all that but I know it won't work, because I'll ask the fatal question:

can I put a piano in the apartment? And the answer is always no. Landladies say no, neighbors say no. I'm commissioned to write a piano concerto but I can't have a piano. No pity on musicians in this city. So I'll have to make it back to Vienna again. Back and forth to Vienna, where they allow pianos."

"Where's Doug?" Simeon asked.

Babe pointed to a blanket where Doug lay talking to a girl with a pretty and very young face. "There he is over there, whisperin' lies into the ears of his unsuspecting French gal."

"I've never seen him with her before."

"He hides her, man. Because she's soft and sweet, and he's afraid that if we see him with her we'll think *he's* soft and sweet, too." Babe chuckled. "As for me, I'm waitin for my i-deel."

Benson said: "Reminds me of the cat who spent all his life looking for the perfect woman to marry. Spent fifty years traveling to every country in the world, never found the woman. Got older and older. Finally, in a little village near his own home city, he saw the ideal woman drawing water from a well. He rushes over to her: 'My love, I've spent all my life looking for the ideal woman; now I've found her, it's you, will you marry me?' and she says: 'Sorry, I'm looking for the ideal man.'"

The music was hypnotic and one of the Brazilian girls stood up and began to dance. Simeon bent and kissed Maria lightly on the mouth. She continued to stare up at the sky and said, "What do you want from me?"

The question surprised him. He said softly, "I want you."

She smiled faintly and was silent again. The wine was in their heads and everyone started to sing with the Brazilians. Carlos shouted that one of the lambs was cooked and began slicing the meat and passing it around. The Brazilian woman danced in a frenzy and they all stopped talking and watched her. A few couples moved off into the woods. The dancing woman circled the fires, her head shining in the firelight, her body gone wild. Simeon watched the faces around the fire, faces ranging from white to brown to black, from Scandinavia to Africa.

Simeon and Maria drove back to Paris with another couple shortly before dawn. Most of the others stayed on, and from the highway Simeon could see the light of the fires against the sky. He was silent and nervous during the drive, terribly aware of Maria's presence. He wanted to sleep with her, but could not fathom her brooding silence. His pride and all of his racial experience made him fear a rebuff if he approached her directly. Yet all that was honest in him had always made him reject any approach but a direct one.

Simeon and Maria got out near Simeon's hotel. "Do you live near here?" Simeon asked.

"Just around the corner. In a hotel."

"Don't go home. Stay with me."

"Yes."

He could have kissed her in gratitude for that rare and beautiful simplicity. Here, thank God, was a woman who played no games.

When, in bed, he touched her body it trembled so violently that he was frightened. She whispered again: "What do you want from me? What do you want?"

2

They slept until early afternoon, then lunched at Marco's, around the corner on the rue des Quatres Vents. Afterward, they went for a walk in the Luxembourg Gardens.

"I feel . . . better," she said, looking at him with a shy smile.

He laughed softly. "So do I."

"But I missed acting school. That is serious."

She hummed gaily, swinging her tall lithe body as she walked, her face bright in the sun. He could not believe she would go blind; she would have a successful operation.

"What are you thinking?" she asked.

"Of how your body swings."

"Better than Brigitte's?"

"Much better."

She laughed. "All men lie."

They returned to Simeon's hotel room in the late afternoon. Maria turned to Simeon with a smile and said, "So we buy an apartment. After all, this room is not big enough for the two of us." She laughed with delight. "I scare you, eh? You are thinking 'Aha, who is this woman who wants to trap me?' Ah yes, you men, you are all the same, my aunt tells me so. Afraid for your precious freedom. Now I must leave you. I must go see my Paris mother."

"When will I see you again? Will you come here tonight?"

"Tonight?" she mocked. "Ah, but is very soon, no? You are sure you are ready for such steady relations? No, we'll protect your freedom. I'll come back in, say, one month."

"Come tonight, Maria."

"Maybe. But I will be late. We are going to Enghein to play roulette. If I do come, I will not be here until four or five in the morning. So that gives you lots of freedom. *Ciaou*, Simeon."

When she had gone, the room seemed empty. He sat at the table and tried to finish a magazine article but felt restless and went downstairs for a beer at Lipp's. He ate alone. He went to a movie after dinner, but could not get Maria out of his thoughts.

He ran into Harold, who said, "Come along with me, I'm going to hear music at a café."

"What café?"

"Come along, you'll see."

Harold led him into a small dingy café, filled with men with curly dark hair and dressed in baggy, unpressed clothes. "Algerians. Arabs," Harold said. From a phonograph came Arab music which had the passion and melancholy of flamenco. The Arabs stared blankly at the two intruders, but the barman, also an Algerian, smiled at Harold and extended his hand.

"*Salud!* Haven't seen you for a long time," he said.

"I was in Vienna. Piano trouble again. Meet Simeon."

They drank cognac at the bar, listening to the music. The Algerians played dominoes or just stared in front of them. They all drank coffee. Simeon knew that there were half a million Algerians in France, but had never before been in one of their cafés. He thought again of the night he had seen a policeman brutalize a man Babe had identified with the laconic comment: "He's probably an Arab."

"There are no women," Simeon said.

Harold said, "The women are at home with their families, in Algeria. The men come here to find work and send money home. People are very poor in Algeria."

They left the café at two o'clock and Harold went home. Simeon went to an all-night bar on the rue Monsieur le Prince where there was a Spanish guitarist. He sat at the bar and ordered a beer. Beside him was a blonde girl reading a Dutch newspaper.

"Could you give me a light?" The girl smiled and held up her cigarette. He struck a match.

"How did you know I speak English?" he asked.

"You dress like an American."

How annoying, Simeon thought. I must buy new clothes. The Dutch girl finished her drink, smiled at him again, and left the bar. Simeon had another beer, and when he went outside it was 3 A.M.

A couple was struggling near a wall. Simeon recognized the Dutch girl, who was being pressed against the wall by a heavy-set man. She was crying and her eyes fell on Simeon.

"Help me! For God's sake, help me, he's going to kill me!" she cried. Simeon hesitated for an instant, then moved toward them and took the man by the shoulder, "This is my fiancée, leave her alone," Simeon said in French.

The man whirled in fury, eyes glaring, and shoved Simeon. "Go away and mind your own business!"

Simeon took a step forward and hit the man on the jaw. The man turned and grappled with Simeon, trying to pull him down to the pavement. Simeon saw the girl run in her high heels down the street, then disappear. He backed away and swung hard, hitting the man flush in the face, this time drawing blood from his lip. The man shouted in a guttural language Simeon recognized as Arabic, and Simeon realized then that the man was Algerian.

The man charged again, butting Simeon hard on the chin with his head; they fell struggling to the ground. Then the door to the bar opened and other men seized Simeon, cursing in Arabic. Simeon was dimly aware of shouts and the screams of women, then suddenly the street was filled with police brandishing tommy guns. "Hands up! Hands up!" the police ordered, shoving the Arabs around roughly. An officer said, "All right, now what's it all about?"

One of the waiters in the bar, who knew Simeon, came forward: "I saw the whole thing. These Arabs attacked the American."

"All right," the officer said, "everybody in the wagon."

The Arabs and Simeon got into the back of the patrol wagon with the police. They sat on wooden benches facing each other. From time to time, one of the policemen cursed and slapped an Algerian in the face. The Arabs stared straight ahead, sullenly. Simeon was embarrassed and confused. He had not realized the man was an Algerian. And the Dutch girl had run off.

The police kept roughing up the Arabs, but they did not touch Simeon. At the police station, they shoved the Algerians through the door. The desk sergeant looked at them with a sigh.

"What happened?" he asked.

"These *bicots* attacked the Monsieur," a policeman said.

The sergeant looked at Simeon. "Do you want to bring charges?"

"No."

"Explain what happened, Monsieur."

The man Simeon had fought tried to speak, but one of the policemen slapped him in the face. The sergeant said to the man, "Be quiet!" then turned to Simeon. "Go ahead, Monsieur." The sergeant had used the familiar *tu* in speaking to the Algerian, but employed the polite *vous* in addressing Simeon.

Simeon felt extremely uncomfortable. He said, "This man was with a girl and, I don't know, I suppose I interfered when I shouldn't have. A fight started, that's all."

The man who had fought Simeon said, "Sergeant, can I talk? Can I explain something?"

The sergeant frowned and looked at his papers. "Go ahead," he said indifferently.

"Sergeant, I was holding the girl to keep her from running. Her name is Thera. I know her, I knew this man wasn't her fiancé because she was *my* girl. She come to my room several times, I took her to bars, spent money on her, she was *my* girl. But listen, Sergeant, I work hard for my money, you know how it is with us here, I work not for me, you understand; I send it to my family in Algeria."

"Get to the point."

"All right. Last Friday I take this girl to my room on payday, when I haven't mailed my money to my family yet. And when I wake up in the morning the girl is gone and my pay is gone! Sergeant, you know what it's like for my family in Algeria without money I send them for one month? I got three kids, I got wife, mother, all kinds of sisters and cousins, they live from money I send them every month. And this bitch walks off with my month's pay! So tonight, when I'm walking down the street, I see her. She wants to run, I hold her against a wall, and I say, 'Look here, you filthy bitch, where's my money! I want my money!' She cries, saying she'll bring me the money some other time, but I don't want to let her out of my sight. Then this guy comes and butts in where it ain't his business and tells a lie that he's her fiancé. This make me mad. *Voilà*."

"That's all you got to say?"

"But, Sergeant, you realize what it's like in Algeria, with no pay for a whole month? You realize?"

The sergeant said, "Listen. *Moi*, I don't feel any pity for you. If you are telling the truth it serves you right for taking that girl home with you. You got no right to molest tourists in this country, you should have stayed in Algeria where you belong." He turned to the police. "Lock him up. And the others, too. A night in jail will do them good."

A policeman said, "The American too?"

"No, not Monsieur."

Simeon looked at the Algerians with a plea for forgiveness. They did not return his glance.

He protested to the sergeant, "But I'm not lodging charges. I didn't know his pay was stolen. They shouldn't be locked up, everything was my fault."

The sergeant frowned. "Listen, are you telling us how to run our own country?"

"No..."

"Okay. Get out of here."

A policeman led Simeon to the entrance. Simeon looked back at the Algerians, who were being pushed roughly through a door in the rear. The policeman put his arm on Simeon's shoulder and said, "You don't understand. You don't know how they are, *les Arabs*. Always stealing, fighting, cutting people, killing. They're a plague; you're a foreigner, you wouldn't know. A night in jail is letting them off easy."

Simeon wandered through the streets before going home at dawn. Maria had not come, but now he was glad to be alone. He lay awake a long time.

3

Just a few months ago in Philadelphia Simeon had left the newspaper office late, and Charlotte, one of the young reporters, said: "Would you mind going with me to the subway? I don't like walking alone at night."

Some people stared as they passed. Charlotte did not

notice this. She was new to the paper and was telling Simeon how exciting she found reporting. Simeon could not help resenting her, as he resented all white friends so secure in their own world as to be blind to the countless storm warnings so acutely detected by the Negro. Charlotte could not see the hatred and threats in the eyes that saw *him* with *her*. "It's what I always dreamed of being," she said. "Maybe it comes from the romantic notions about reporting you get from the movies." She had an infectious laugh and was likable, but Simeon was irritated that she was enjoying life so fully in the nation that made life so difficult for him.

"Thanks," she said when they got to the subway. "Do you have a minute? Let me buy you a drink." Simeon nodded and they went into a bar. Charlotte continued: "But what I really like is feature writing. I'm doing some free-lance stuff. Maybe you'll read it for me one of these days."

There was a group of white sailors at a table in the bar. They were looking at Simeon and Charlotte and whispering among themselves. Their eyes were not friendly. "Sure," Simeon said. "Although I haven't done much magazine work myself. The main thing for magazines is to write anecdotes. Fill your article with a lot of anecdotes, nothing but anecdotes." A couple of the sailors stood up and moved in the direction of the door behind Simeon. "Yes, anecdotes," Charlotte said. "A magazine article is like a string of beads: each bead is an anecdote, and the string is the connecting idea." As they passed, one of the sailors suddenly whirled and hit Simeon on the jaw with all his strength. Charlotte screamed. The other sailors rushed forward, cursing and swinging at Simeon. Rage burned with the pain in Simeon's head, and as he looked at the nearest sailor, the hallucination returned: *It was the stone face!* It was Chris-Mike. He leaped free of the sailors and drew the pistol he always carried now. He looked at them, at their suddenly frightened faces, smiled, and pulled the trigger.

The gun jammed. The sailors, the barman, and all the customers stared at him in amazement. "Let's get out of here," Charlotte whispered. She ran to the door while Simeon, the gun pointed toward the sailors, backed swiftly out of the bar.

On the street he ran as he had never run before. He jumped onto a moving bus. He could hardly breathe. He was so weak that he almost collapsed, and his hand trembled violently as he paid. The conductor stared at him curiously, and Simeon got off the bus before his stop. He walked down a small dark street, took the pistol from his pocket, wiped it carefully with his handkerchief and tossed it into a sewer. He stood in the street a moment, shaking. *I almost committed a murder.*

In bed that night he forced himself to be calm. But the face—of Mike, of Chris, of the sailor—would not leave his mind. "You're going off your rocker," he told himself. Murder in a bar, then the electric chair, what a ridiculous way to end life! To die for a cause, that would be one thing. But in a barroom brawl!

He told himself slowly and lucidly: *I'm going to kill a man someday.* In a moment of anger, humiliation, an instant of illusion, of hallucination. No! Not that waste, not kill himself through his own irrational act!

He would go away, leave America. Go where? Anywhere. Europe, for example. France.

Simeon slept fitfully, aware of the Paris street sounds. At four in the afternoon he got up and went to a bar. He ordered a beer, then another. He did not feel like eating, and started to wander aimlessly along the Boulevard St. Germain. He was passing near the Metro Odéon when he heard a voice shout in thickly accented English: "Hey! How does it feel to be a white man?"

Simeon knew somehow that the words were for him and, turning, saw four Algerians sitting at a table of the Odéon Café. Confused and humble, Simeon walked over to them.

"Sit down," one man said, studying Simeon with a bitter mocking smile. Two of the other men stared at Simeon with open hostility while the fourth, who looked younger than the rest, looked at him with curiosity, even sympathy. "What're you drinking?"

"Coffee," Simeon answered.

The man who spoke English ordered the coffee, then turned to Simeon. "Well? How does it feel?"

Simeon shrugged. "I didn't realize."

The man leaned toward Simeon and said angrily, "You didn't realize! Listen, I was with the Free French during the war. Got a decoration. For a time, I was with the Navy and I went to the States. Where you from?"

"Philadelphia."

"Yeah, I been to Philadelphia. Baltimore, too. New York. Went with the Free French, I believed the stuff they were saying during the war, you know; that afterward the world would be different, it was a war for democracy, we were all fighting for democracy and freedom. Big words. Stupid, huh? Nice, the States. I saw how they treated people like you there, black people. Went to neighborhoods where Negroes lived, had Negro friends. Fine how they treated black people, huh? What was the word they used? *Niggers.* That's what they called you, ain't it? Niggers! Yeah, I saw. And guess what—in the States, they considered *me* and people like me white! But I wasn't fooled, I went to the black neighborhoods anyway."

He chuckled, then went on. "Well, how do you feel now? Feel fine, huh? Over here in the France, land of the free. Far away from the stuff back in the States, huh? Can go anyplace, do anything. That's great. I remember how it was back there. If a white man fought a black man, the black man was guilty, the white man was innocent. Just like that. I remember. How does it feel to have the roles reversed, eh? How does it feel to be the white man for a change?"

Simeon shook his head, wanting to get up and walk away, but the Algerian was relentless: "We're the niggers here! Know what the French call us—*bicot, melon, raton, nor'af.* That means *nigger* in French. Ain't you scared we might rob you? Ain't you appalled by our unpressed clothes, our body odor? No, but seriously, I want to ask you a serious question—would you let your daughter marry one of us?"

The torrent of words was suddenly stopped by the man's harsh laughter. Then he said wearily: "It's okay. You didn't know, maybe. It's okay. But think next time."

"Yes."

"Don't let there be no next time."

"There won't be any next time."

"Okay. Take off. Take off. We don't want you with us. Take off."

"Let's . . . have a drink."

"No, no, take off."

He hesitated, but they had slammed the door in his face. He stood up. "See you around," he said.

As he walked off, the Algerian shouted: "You hear? No next time, white man!"

V

I

SIMEON dreamed he sailed the ocean, crossed the sea to visit the Folks, Them Folks and Our Folks, and parents of soft harsh distant caresses. Native land. Once there he was broke, he did not have enough money to return to Paris.

"It's wonderful," his mother said, "you'll be with us longer. And if you work hard, in a few years you'll save enough money to make a trip back to France."

He doubled up like a fetus on the floor and wailed as though his heart would explode, while his three brothers and two sisters and his cousins and aunts and uncles patted him on the shoulder and said, "You can go see Frances, your old girlfriend. She hasn't married yet, maybe she'll have you." He wailed like a baby, like Arab music.

Words, spoken by an old, old man with beard: "Son, wherever racism exists, wherever oppression exists, anybody who lives complacently in its shadow is guilty and damned forever!"

Wailed, until the doctors came and carried him away to the police station. Chris smiled, brushing a speck from his uniform. "Them French are dirty," he said soothingly. "Besides, they're nigger-lovers. Ain't you glad to be back among us?" The eye socket screamed as acid flowed.

He tossed and turned, between sleep and consciousness. His father said, "Ain' no son of mine supposed..."

What was his father like? Warm summer evenings when morale was good, his father was a tall broad man with black skin and narrow eyes and a jagged scar on his cheek. Silent and fierce. *"Tell us what it was like, Papa."* Stories of the old days, how it was. How he revolted with the slaves, revolted with Denmark Vesey and Gabriel and Nat Turner, fought them Crackers, saw the blood flow, saw his brothers fall, but fought all the same. Ain' gonna let no white folks hold us down! Lynchings. Riots. They had to form the Ku Klux Klan to hold us down, son. Had to hide their faces behind masks, had to come sneaking in the night, armed with guns, while we was there naked with our bare hands, son. Still couldn't hold us down, son. Nobody can't hold us down.

"Tell us how it was, Papa." Cold winter nights when morale was low, Papa was a small man with soft, hurting eyes. Reed bending in the wind. Ole darky with bowed head, smiling white teeth and red gums, humiliated, smiling despite the humiliation, in order to survive. How was it, Papa? Singing songs to ole Massa, singing songs to put ole Massa to sleep. Waiting and watching. To survive.

"Sons," the old man said, leaning back from his throat-burning drink and looking with old eyes toward the ceiling, "I was riding a bus in the South, riding a Jim Crow bus, and I was young then, and I was proud. And there wasn't no seats in the colored section, so I stood at the borderline between the colored section and the white section, and a white man come in and took the seat in the white section next to where I was standing. He looked at me. His eyes was tired and there was blood in them. He looked at me and said, 'Nigger, what you doing standing here in the white section?' I said, 'Sir,

I'm not standing in the white section, I'm standing on the borderline.' 'Move back a step,' the white man said, and I did. Now, the man's eyes was tired, and there was blood in them. He looked at me and I saw the blood and the tiredness, and I saw the pain and the fright, and he saw me looking and he reached in his pocket and pulled out a pack of cigarettes. 'Nigger,' he said, 'open this pack of cigarettes for me.' He held the cigarettes up toward me. The bus was quiet; everybody was looking to see if I'd open the cigarettes. I looked at the cigarettes and I didn't move. I was young, then, and I was proud, and I decided it was time to die. The man's face got red. 'Nigger, you hear a white man telling you to do something? Open them cigarettes!' I didn't move. I saw the white folks and the colored folks looking, waiting. Through the mirror, I saw the bus driver grin and slip his hand back to touch the handle of his pistol, waiting.

"Now, there was an old, old colored woman with proud eyes and proud head sitting on the seat just in front of me. She looked at me with a smile, and said softly, 'Son, open the man's cigarettes for him. Go 'head,' she coaxed gently. I was mad, but I did what she said. The white man grinned. 'That's a good nigger.' The white folks on the bus looked peculiar, the bus driver sort of frowned. The old lady looked at me and patted my hand and winked, and suddenly I *knew*. The colored folks on the bus had their jaws set and their eyes were mad; they were mad again, but they looked at me and smiled and winked. *They knew*. That ole Jim Crow bus drove on."

When his mother worked as maid for white people on Chestnut Street, she used to sleep in and come home only on Tuesdays, her day off. Simeon always looked forward to that day. One Tuesday she didn't come home. He tried to be brave but he couldn't help it and cried. Papa said, "Ain' no son of mine supposed to cry." But Papa was sad, too. She came home on Wednesday instead, and explained: "See, Tuesday was voting day. And Mrs. Delaney (that was the rich white woman she worked for), Mrs. Delaney, she asked me, 'Sarah, you gonna vote?' 'Yes ma'am,' I said. 'Who you gonna vote for, Sarah?' And I said, 'Why, I'm gonna vote for Mister Roosevelt, Mrs. Delaney, he done done a lot for my people.' Mrs. Delaney looked real mad. She said, 'Well, tell you what, Sarah, me and Mr. Delaney, we don't like Roosevelt, and we don't want him to have no votes, so you won't vote today. You'll work, you hear me, you won't have no time to go to the polls and commit no foolishness. Shouldn'ta give the vote to colored anyway!'"

Simeon listened, amazed. He listened, eyes big and round, astonished. Then he swore on his honor: "Mama, when I'm big, I'm gonna change things, I'm gonna have a lot of money and I'm gonna change things so you won't never have to take orders from no white people no more. You hear?"

"Hello, white man," his brother said, driving a pick into the soil. All of his brothers were there.

He, Simeon, was dressed in a tuxedo, wearing a bow tie and a red carnation in his lapel. The brothers were in rags, smelling of stale sweat. All of them were blind, their pupils rolled back into their heads, only the whites of their eyes showing. Motionless, blind, yet they all seemed to see him.

He saw his own face, that of a pale zombie, in the mirror. He had two eyes again. The brothers swung picks, working the soil, sweating, breathing hard.

One of his brothers was tied with a hangman's rope to a tree in their yard. A tiger circled the brother. The brother watched in horrified fascination. The tiger bared its fangs and hissed and leaped. The brother cried to Simeon: *"Die with me!"*

2

One day at the Touron, Simeon asked Raoul and Henri, two French students he knew: "Is there racism in France?"

Raoul said quickly, "Of course not. The French don't believe in racist theories; everybody knows that. Africans feel perfectly at home here. The French don't *understand* racism. Why do you ask?"

"What about Arabs?"

Raoul hesitated, frowning. Then his smooth voice said, "That's different. The French don't like the Arabs, but it's not racism. The Arabs don't like us either. We're different."

"It's a difference with you on top and them on the bottom."

"That's a historical accident."

"It's always a historical accident in the beginning. Why do you say you're different?"

Raoul waved his hands helplessly. "They're a closed people. You can't really get to know them. They scowl when you laugh; you never know what they're thinking. And if you turn your back, they're liable to stick a knife in it."

"I've heard that kind of argument before."

"It's different. I assure you it's not racism."

Henri shook his head. "Cut it out, Raoul. That's nonsense. The French are racists as far as the Algerians are concerned, no doubt about it."

Raoul's eyes flashed. "How can you say that?"

Henri shrugged. "Why try to say anything different? The

French are prejudiced, they don't think of Algerians as human beings. Especially the middle classes."

"Let's not start the class war again."

"Have you ever invited an Arab to your home?"

"There are *lots* of people I've never invited to my home!"

"Do you have any Arab friends? Would you even *consider* the possibility of having a serious conversation with an Arab? Don't you resent it when an Arab sits at a table next to you in a café, or beside you in the bus? If you were renting out a room in your apartment, would you even *consider* renting it to an Arab? No, it's racism, Raoul. Let's face it."

"It's not racism. They're *different*. I wouldn't rent a room to an Arab because he'd probably rob the whole apartment while I was out. That's a fact. But it's not racism."

Simeon suppressed a smile, and said nothing.

PART TWO
The White Man

I

I

THE TALL, stout man with balding head walked down the path toward Simeon and Maria. They were sitting on a bench in the Luxembourg Gardens. The stout man halted a couple of yards in front of them and stared. Simeon suddenly felt himself going tense. He looked up at the man's red intent face, but the man did not move.

Maria did not seem to notice anything. Simeon continued to glare, but the man did not move or alter his gaze. Brazen bastard, Simeon thought. Never saw a black man and a white woman before? This is Paris, man! Simeon jumped to his feet.

"What's the matter, man, see something you don't like?"

"Bitte?" the man said, startled. "Please? I am sorry. Is difficult to understand English. You are American? I am Cherman."

German. Well, everyone knew *their* racial ideas! Still, the fact that the man was not an American calmed Simeon somewhat.

"What're you staring at?"

"Staring? Ah I'm sorry. Is just—your young lady has such a remarkable face. The glasses and all, with the bones, you see. I am painter. I was fascinated. Forgive me. I did not mean to stare." He smiled, bowed stiffly, turned and walked off.

Simeon sat down, his hands trembling. He felt ridiculous; the man was a painter! Maria was looking at him in surprise.

"Why did you talk to him so rough? He did nothing."

Simeon shrugged nervously. She had not understood.

"It's just that he was staring so hard."

She laughed. "Staring? But that hurts no one. It is flattering, in fact. It is no reason to be angry."

He was furious with himself, but more furious with her for not understanding.

"No. Only in the States. It's complicated..."

No she could not understand. He often felt far away from her emotionally and now deliberately pushed her farther into that alien white world. The incident with the Algerians had changed his attitude toward life in Paris—he was more conscious of the distance between himself and the other white people around him, including the French. There has been a return of buried hatreds; forgotten walls had shot up again between him and the world.

2

The air was hot and dusty under the trees in the Gardens as Maria and Simeon walked on. The slow sensuousness of Maria's walk excited him. She was staring with a wistful envy at the children playing ball, sailing boats. But she was more than a child, Simeon thought. She was a prism of changing moods. Very often in her sleep she moaned and talked in Polish. Sometimes she screamed, then woke up.

"Are you all right, Maria?"

"Is the light on?" she'd say in terror.

"No." He flicked the switch. She closed her eyes and

sobbed in relief, her head on his shoulder. For an instant, Simeon knew, she had thought she was blind.

Was she ever really a self he could grasp, identify? In the act of love? He had always been shy; even in the days of the Chase, he could rarely lose consciousness of himself. But Maria had no shyness, no inhibitions of this sort. Her body gave itself completely and her passion had the power of thawing Simeon, melting the frozen muscles. This lovely child-woman who did not understand him and whom he did not understand.

3

They lunched, then took a nap early in the afternoon. Simeon woke before Maria, slipped on his clothes and went out to have a cup of coffee and buy a newspaper. When he came back, Maria was sitting up in the bed, furiously exhaling the smoke of a cigarette. Her legs were covered, her waist and breasts bare, and her dark, fragile eyes were staring at the wall straight ahead.

"Awake at last?" Simeon said cheerfully. "Hello."

She did not reply and would not look at him.

"What's the matter?" Simeon said.

"You are one of such men!"

"One of what men?"

"*You* know what sort of men! Those who must always seduce the maids in hotels!"

Simeon was stunned and wanted to laugh, but her face was so wrought with anger and pain that he did not have the heart. "My sweet Slavic soul," he said, "let's start at the beginning. What man? What maid? What are we talking about?"

She looked at him now, as though a first doubt were gleaming in her mind. "I heard her, the maid. She met a man in the hall, I could tell it was you, and they laughed and began whispering together and then went together into the empty room across the hall. I knew it was you! Don't lie. I wanted to go throw open the door and scratch out her eyes, and yours, too, but I was too proud. So I sat here smoking and waiting. Five minutes ago they came out, and whispered and laughed again. And I waited. And now, here you are. Pretending to be innocent!"

This time Simeon did laugh. She looked at him and frowned, still uncertain. "I never even saw the maid. I was downstairs, buying a paper and having a coffee."

"I don't believe you!"

"Here's the paper." He held up a copy of the London *Observer*. Maria, still frowning, stamped her cigarette out in the ashtray, then stared again at the wall. Finally she threw off the covers and walked toward the washstand. As she passed him, she grinned sheepishly and kissed him lightly on the mouth.

Simeon lay across the bed and admired her long legs and high, uptilting breasts. Her skin was bronzed and smooth to the touch, not waxen like the skin of Ingrid the Swedish girl. Naked, Maria always moved him to a tender, protective feeling.

He said, "And now explain, *mon trésor*. Where did you hear about 'such men' as sleep with maids in hotels?"

"I read about it."

"Where?"

"In ... French novels I read in Poland."

He laughed. He adored her. He wanted suddenly to kiss her, to commit himself, place himself in her power. But he was afraid of her. He knew he could easily become the slave of that somber face and long careless body. He was certain he would lose her one day to another world.

He laughed and said, "And you think of me like the people in those novels? *Me?* And I'm not French!"

She raised a leg to wash a foot in the washbasin. "No, but you live in Paris. You are one of these Paris men. Sophisticated. Many women before."

He studied her mobile face in the mirror. She was so full of contradictions. She was shy in company, yet on hot summer days she liked to wear only a thin dress without underclothes. When Simeon raised an eyebrow she would shrug and say: "It's too hot; I want to be comfortable." She was careful with money, but at the Enghein gambling casino she would throw away hundreds of thousands of her Paris mother's francs on a turn of the wheel. He had not taken her aspirations to be an actress seriously until he went to see her in Lorca's *Noces de Sang*. He had received a shock seeing her without her glasses in the role of the Fiancée, dressed in a Spanish costume. She was electric and convincing.

Now she studied herself critically in the mirror. She had completely forgotten her accusation about the maid.

He said with mock solemnity, "Now, Maria, I want the truth. How many men have you slept with?"

She frowned "Slept with? Lovers?" She turned and looked at him and, as always, he could not tell what was behind the film over her eyes. "Two men, Simeon. You are the second man. This is the truth. But there is something else. I cannot tell you now. I tell you another time.... And you? How many women?"

"I don't know."

"A guess."

"I couldn't even guess. Honestly. I can't remember about when I was young."

She laughed. "You are still young. Looking at yourself with your black patch in mirror, like a little boy pirate. I bet you had this fantasy when you were a child."

"Yes."

"I as a child always imagined I was an actress. As a child in Poland, in German labor camp, my mind was always far away in America or France." She looked at the unfinished portrait of the monstrous white face, which Simeon had propped on the easel. "Why you paint such a terrible face?" she asked. "It looks like somebody I knew before."

Simeon stood up and looked at the portrait. What are they doing now, he wondered—Chris, Mike, the sailor? "No," he said firmly. He removed the canvas from the frame, rolled it up and snapped a rubber band around it, and tossed it into a closet.

"You should burn it," she said.

"No. I want to keep it."

She dressed and they went out. Simeon said, "I want to take you someplace. Show you something."

"What is it?"

"I've found an apartment."

It was a studio apartment on the rue Saint-Sulpice, just around the corner from his hotel. He had paid three months rent in advance, and could move on the first of the month.

The apartment consisted of a large, light studio, a smaller room, kitchen and bath.

"Do you like it?" Simeon asked.

"Very much."

He felt awkward. "Maria, there's not much sense in your

keeping your room while I have this apartment. Come live here with me."

She laughed. "Ah, and your male freedom!"

"I'll be free enough."

She looked out of the window. Her face had changed again. "No, I think it is better for both of us, especially for you, if I keep my room." She looked at him and smiled. "But I bring toothbrush here, if you like. And bedroom slippers. That way, if you bring another woman here, she knows you belong to me!"

Late in the afternoon they strolled along the Seine and through the Tuileries and then along the Champs-Élysées. It was a splendid warm day, the café terraces were filled, children played in the parks and hundreds of people were also out walking. Simeon always felt an intense pleasure when he walked through Paris. How had this miracle happened? Why wasn't he back on South Street, in the sweltering slums, where he belonged? He felt both happy and uneasy.

"Champs-Élysées!" Maria said. "Since I was child, and read about in books, I dreamed how I would love walking on this street."

She stopped at every shopwindow, staring happily at everything from women's clothes to automobiles. When well-dressed women passed, she would squeeze Simeon's hand. "Look at that beautiful dress! The woman is so elegant! I would like to be like her!"

"She's probably shallow, conceited, stupid..."

"Maybe. But such clothes! And the way she walks! She probably has a big house and cars and servants!"

He sometimes found himself wondering whether Maria ever thought of anything else. And then he remembered the murmurings, the sobs at night.

They sat on the terrace of Fouquet's, ordered coffee and commented on the passing world of the Champs-Élysées. A group of Africans walked by; they saw Simeon, smiled, and nodded a greeting. Simeon felt warm inside. Black men nearly always greeted black men on the streets of Paris. They knew each other.

"What did you do in America?" Maria asked suddenly.

"I worked for a newspaper."

"You made much money?"

"Compared to French standards, yes."

She shook her head. "I can't understand why you left. Oh, I like Paris very much, but I think I will always have little money here. But in the United States, I will make a lot of money and have car. I asked you before why you left, and you told me was because life there was gray. Why did you really go?"

He did not really want to talk about it with Maria, but tried. "I got tired of waiting for the dream to come true."

"*Comment?*"

"I'm impatient. I didn't like the big and little humiliations of being a black man there."

She frowned, looking toward the street. "I don't understand it. I read some things about it, you know, what happens there with the race problem. But I don't understand it. Is it really so terrible, still?"

"You mean, do they chase black men down the streets of Philadelphia and New York with lynch ropes? No. And in an ordinary day, nothing striking happens, people don't even notice you on the street. But a hundred tiny things happen—micro-particles, nobody can see them but us. And there's always the danger that something bigger will happen. The Beast in the Jungle, you're always tense, waiting for it to spring. It's terrible, yes. And, we want to breathe air, we don't want to think about this race business twenty-four hours a day. We don't want our noses pushed down in it for the seventy-odd years of our lives. But you have to keep thinking about it; they force you to think about it all the time."

"Aren't you ever going back?"

"I don't know." He was surprised at his uncertainty. It had not occurred to him before that he might never return to America. He was struck by the irony of being with a woman who longed to go to the country he had fled. Still, there was a similarity in their pasts and, in the present, they were fugitives. Paris was a way-station for both of them, and neither could predict anything beyond the present moment.

Simeon felt close to Maria that night, as she lay in bed smoking a cigarette and looking at the cream-colored ceiling through those condemned eyes, saying, "What you asked me this afternoon, about how many men I slept with before, yes, I must tell you. I said you were the second man. Second *normal* man, you understand. First was a Polish man I knew."

"Who is he?" Simeon asked, jealously.

"He was the man that I was going to marry, but it could not work. He is *builder*, enthusiastic about building Poland up from the ruins. I admire him, but I wanted to flee, you understand." Her fingers gently touched his patch. "My poor Simeon, your eye . . . my eyes . . . our eyes bring us together, perhaps."

"Perhaps."

"But before you and before the other man there was the war and the labor camp where I was with my parents during the Occupation, and there was a German officer. When I was nine years old. It was not exactly that he made love to me; he had—odd tastes. I am ashamed. . . . You understand, we were so hungry, so cold, so miserable and frightened, we became horrible people, we would do anything to stay alive. You must never see people brought so low, Simeon; you see what we are capable of and it is terrible, savage. . . . The German officer, the camp commander, liked me. I did what he wanted to keep me and my parents alive.

"I went to his quarters often. I was there often when the officers met and drank and ate and talked. He was strange, the commander. Many times you could think he was an ordinary human being, with human feelings; but then, at times, something would seem to go click inside him, especially when he was drunk. His face would change. I cannot describe it; it was terrible—yes, like the face in your portrait; his eyes would be hard, the blood would go away and his skin would be white like ashes, cold like stone. At such moments he was cruel, and would smile when he could humiliate or kill or cause pain.

"You know what is the 'line-up'? From time to time, they called out all the prisoners of the camp and the commander passed, saying, 'You, step to the right; you, step to the left,' until all of the prisoners had been formed into two lines. Then one of the lines was led away, and we never saw those people again. We knew they had gone to the gas chambers. What was terrible was that you never knew *which* of the two lines would be led away. And each person hoped that the *other* line would be led away, no matter who was in it; it was horrible how one wanted to stay alive, how one wanted the *others* to die so one could stay alive!

"Now, me, after a time, I knew I did not have to worry, for I could feel that the commander was a bit in love with me, and I knew that the line where he put me and my parents would never be led away. But one night, when I was in his rooms, he was very strange. He had received a letter from Germany, and he read it over and over, and at one point I saw tears in his eyes. Very strange, tears in those cold eyes. He looked at me suddenly almost with hate and said, 'You, you think you know something about suffering! What can you Poles know!' And he sent me away.

"The next morning there was a line-up. When the commander came, I could see that he was very drunk and that he had not slept all night. He walked among the prisoners, saying, 'To the right, to the left.' I was standing between my mother and father. When he came to me, he said, 'You, to the right,' and then he said to my father and to my mother, 'You, to the left.' I screamed. The commander turned and stared at me as though he could kill me. I ran to him and whispered, 'My parents, my parents, you put them in the other line!' He looked at me as though he did not know me, then pushed me away and walked on, saying, 'To the right, to the left.' I screamed, I screamed, I was hysterical, but my father called to me: 'Be brave, Maria, little Maria.' My mother was crying, too. Then the commander gave the order that the line with my parents be marched away.

"My father smiled and threw a kiss and said his last words to me: 'Turn around, Maria, turn your back and don't look at us. You must not look. You must not look.' I didn't want to do it, but at the same time I didn't want to see, you understand? I turned. I was crying, and I kept thinking, 'I have now seen them for the last time! They are right there behind me, but I have seen them for the last time!' I heard the line move off and I screamed with all my voice, but I did not look back, I did not turn around. Then suddenly I realized that I had not said good-by to them. I turned around, but the line was gone. I fell down on the ground, and all I could think was, 'I did not even say good-by.'"

Simeon was silent. He held her tight, feeling more close to her than ever. Perhaps they could understand each other, after all. He watched the smoke of their cigarettes curl upward to the ceiling. Maria kissed his shoulder and said, "You understand, Simeon, I do not tell you this for pity. Millions of people lived the same. But this is part of me, you must understand it to understand me. For years, after the war, I dreamed of nothing except that camp, that line-up, the faces of my parents and the face of that commander. For years I dreamed how I could torture and kill that man. For years, I could not sleep unless there was a knife under my pillow. You understand? And now, I don't want to think about it. I don't want to think about anything. For my sanity, I want to pretend it never happened. Only to you I tell this."

II

I

SIMEON was stretched out in a chair, his long legs extended in front of him, having an after-dinner coffee on the terrace of La Chope with Lou, Clyde, and some of the Brazilians.

It was evening and Clyde had been drinking heavily as usual all day long. He looked at them with bloodshot eyes. "That goddamn Jinx. Wonder where she is. All I ever know about that bitch is that she's in a bed someplace with somebody else."

Simeon said, "Great love between you two. By the way, what do you do with your daughter?"

Clyde's eyes opened wide. "Jinx takes her with her. That's the honest-to-God truth. Has the kid wait downstairs in the lobby, or in a café next door! You ever heard of a mother like that?" He stared at his glass, his blond mustache twitching, lost in unsteady thought. He jerked his head up and looked at Simeon again, as though remembering something. "You're a good boy, Simeon. A real buddy. I like you, know that? When we get back to the States, want you to come see me, meet my folks."

"Yeah, I can just see myself ringing your doorbell down there in Georgia or wherever you come from, Clyde."

"No, no, I'm sincere. Want you to visit us. Be pals, just like over here."

The ancient buildings of the Place de la Contrescarpe sagged, as though about to collapse outward. An orange moon hung overhead, lighting the trees, the smelly pissoir and the lounging tramps. The air vibrated with the noise of motors, voices, pinball machines and the rock-'n-roll of a juke box.

Simeon stretched and glanced into the café, and an Algerian standing at the bar smiled and waved to him. The face seemed familiar, but Simeon could not place the young man. He stood up and went inside.

"You don't recognize me?" the man asked in French. "I was in the bar when you had a fight with an Algerian, and I was sitting on the terrace the next day when Hossein called to you—the man who called you a white man. Remember?"

"Oh, I remember all right," Simeon said with a nervous laugh. A faint echo of the shame returned. He remembered the man now—the only one of the Algerians on the terrace who had looked at him with a degree of sympathy.

"My name's Ahmed. Do you have a minute? What will you drink? I was hoping I'd run into you again."

They sat down. An old woman sitting at a nearby table sniffed in disapproval. An echo of America, Simeon thought, enraged at the woman's contempt for Ahmed.

Ahmed looked somewhat like Simeon. He had the same thin face, deep brown eyes; he was tall, with long, nervous hands. But his skin was swarthy, not black, and his hair, though very curly, was not the hair of a Negro.

Simeon asked, "Why did you want to see me again?"

Ahmed said apologetically. "Hossein was too hard on you. You looked so sad and hurt. I wanted to tell you that everything is all right. After all, you could not know how things were with us."

"I know now."

"Yes. That's good."

Ahmed's eyes were wide and candid. He smiled constantly as he talked, gesturing in an apologetic way, while his eyes never left Simeon's face. He leaned forward, attentive and concerned whenever Simeon spoke.

He said, "I am glad we met here. I have never talked to a black American before. I felt sympathetic to you when I saw you that first time. I told Hossein, 'How can you talk to this man this way, he has a black skin.' And Hossein replied, 'He is a black *American*. This means he thinks like a white man.'"

Ahmed leaned forward, smiling shyly. "What I liked—perhaps it was because I felt we were similar in some way."

"Perhaps. In what way?"

"Something gentle." He watched Simeon's face, as if afraid he might offend him. Reassured, he went on, "You looked sensitive. Someone repelled by hatred and violence."

Simeon smiled. "Yes, we could be very much alike in that way."

"You understand, I know some people who have acquired a taste for it, for the violence and the hate. The Foreign Legionnaires in Algeria, they are like this. Men from all countries, they enjoy to pillage and rape and torture and kill. Their eyes shine with joy. Some police here in France are like this, also. We are not like this."

He studied Simeon's face, to make certain he was being understood. Ahmed seemed to be talking about something that obsessed him. "You understand me, violence, brutality, they must be sometimes used when there is no other way. The way we are fighting this war is necessary—there is no escape.

But one must not acquire the taste for it. This has bothered me; I do not like the terrorism, the killing and the planting of bombs. They are necessary, we act really in self-defense. You as a black man in America, you must have been angry many times, but I am sure you did not *like* to hate all the time. Hossein likes it, hating the French. But you and me, we are different from him. In our hatred of violence, we are alike."

Ahmed sipped his coffee. Simeon remembered that Moslems rarely drank alcohol. Ahmed continued, "My brother does not like violence, but he uses it. He is in Algeria with an army unit of the FLN—the Algerian National Liberation Front. You have heard of it?"

"There's nothing else in the newspapers."

"*Four years* my brother has been in the mountains fighting! Wounded seven times, still he fights. Any day, I expect to receive news that he is dead. Two of my cousins are dead, the others and my father and uncles are dead or disappeared in the camps, we don't know which. I should be there in the mountains, too. I tell myself that all the time, I should be there. Anyway, I am a student, and the FLN tells me I must get my education, they will need trained men when Algeria becomes free. I do some things here . . . little things. But it's not enough." He laughed suddenly, seeming very young when his face became animated. "I'm just a bourgeois intellectual! That's what some of my friends tell me. It's what Hossein thinks."

"What do you study?"

"Medicine. And I write, I want to be a writer." He frowned. "But that seems so useless when so many people are dying."

They left the café together. Lou, Clyde and the Brazilians

were no longer on the terrace. Ahmed said, "Which way do you go?"

"Toward the Luxembourg."

"We can go part of the way together."

They followed a narrow street. Simeon was relieved to have talked with Ahmed. Hossein's words had stuck in his mind. Talking to Ahmed seemed to set things right again. He hummed to himself the spiritual:

> I went to the rock to hide my face;
> The rock cried out, "No hiding place,
> No hiding place down here."

They circled the Panthéon and passed in front of a police station. A policeman stood guard outside, standing behind a shoulder-high concrete shelter, a submachine gun in his hand. He stared at Ahmed and Simeon.

As they neared the corner, Ahmed said with a smile, "Every time I go by that police station at night, alone or with other Algerians, the guard points that gun at me and orders me inside. They check my papers and ask what I'm doing out so late at night. They have sweet words for me, like *bicot* or *melon*, then shove me on my way. Every time."

"And why didn't they do it tonight?" Simeon asked, suspecting the answer.

"Because I'm with you. With someone who looks 'respectable.'" He laughed. "How does it feel, being respectable?"

"Odd."

"And having so much power?"

"Odd. The oddest thing in the world."

They halted at the corner before separating. Ahmed said,

"How about having dinner with me tomorrow night? We could eat *couscous* in an Algerian restaurant."

"Great."

They arranged to meet at the Tournon at seven.

2

Orpheus descending into Harlem, Simeon thought. At the bus stop the next day, Joey the Drunk staggered toward them, staring at Ahmed with curiosity. Joey was a gray-haired American Negro with bloodshot eyes who had been in Paris since the end of the war and worked as a waiter in a Pigalle night club. He scowled at Simeon.

"Hey, man, need five hundred. You got it?"

Babe had said that nobody in Paris could ever remember having seen Joey sober. Nor had anyone ever seen him smile.

"Yeah." Simeon gave Joey a five-hundred-franc bill.

Joey took the money angrily. He reeked of alcohol. "This don't mean I'm poor," he said aggressively. "I just don't have no money on me."

"Sure, sure."

"I'll pay you back when I run across you next time."

"Okay," Simeon said, kissing the bill good-by.

The bus moved northward from the student quarter. They passed the Palace of Justice, the crowded street in front of the Sarah Bernhardt Theater, the gray office buildings of the Bourse area, Les Grands Boulevards. Ghosts of the great cafés where painters and journalists had argued passionately; now a popular neighborhood for Sunday strollers, complete with shooting galleries and sidewalk booths.

Northward toward the Harlem. The further north the

bus moved, the more drab became the buildings, the streets and the people. Cheap stores selling clothes, furniture, kitchen utensils: "Easy terms, ten months to pay!" Cafés became dimmer, the streets narrower and noisier, more and more children filled the sidewalks. Men out of work, with nothing to do and no place to go, stood in sullen, futile groups on street corners. Arab music blared from the dark cafés or from the open windows of bleak hotels. Then suddenly, police were everywhere, stalking the streets, eyes moving insolently from face to face, submachine guns strung from their shoulders.

It was like Harlem, Simeon thought, except that there were fewer cops in Harlem, but maybe that too would come one day. Like Harlem and like all the ghettos of the world. The men he saw through the window of the bus had whiter skins and less frizzly hair, but they were in other ways like the Negroes in the United States. They adopted the same poses: "stashing" on corners, ready for and scared of the ever-possible "trouble," eyes sullen and distrusting, dressed in pegged pants, flashy shirts and narrow pointed shoes. He could almost hear them saying: "Whatchu puttin down, man?" "Jus' playin it cool, jus' playin it cool, man, tryin to keep ole Charlie off my back." Ole Charlie paced the street, waving his submachine gun. Simeon watched everything, remembering how it was on South Street and Lombard Street, feeling the old unbearable frustration and anger, the fear and defiance. Who knew anything about all this? What did *Them Folks* know about this or that or about anything? Who was alive except us down here, us here down under, feeling the heat and weight of what life was in the all-too-real present, watching ghostly clowns play frivolous games there above? Street vendors shouted their wares in Arabic: fruit, clothes, vegetables. He remembered the pushcarts in his childhood on Tenth Street, the sweating men plugging holes in watermelons so you could taste them, opening fish and cleaning them and scaling them for you, shouting in the mornings, "Any old rags, any papers, any iron?" The odors of rotting food and of cooking mingled in the air, and he remembered how they had smelled to him—the fried chicken or the greens, the uncollected garbage in the alleys and gutters. Arab music assailed them from all sides. The Blues. Where was the Blues Singer now? In the dismal cafés, men played pinball or football machines, or stood at counters staring at nothing, empty coffee cups in front of them. There were no women. The police paced the streets, their faces hard.

Simeon was aware that Ahmed was staring at him, boyish and intent, searching for his reactions, just as he had that day when Hossein had called to Simeon.

"Where are you?" Ahmed asked.

"Home."

They got out of the bus and wove their way slowly through the crowded, narrow streets to a big café-restaurant. Simeon felt immediately conspicuous in his well-pressed American suit and starched white collar. Men in shabby pants and worn tennis shoes stared at him, their gazes not hostile but questioning. You never knew in a jungle world. One of the Algerians was almost as brown as Simeon, but you could tell by the eyes and the hair that the man was not Negro. Harlem! Harlem! Simeon felt disappointed, as if he had really expected all of the Algerians to break into smiles and rush to embrace him shouting: "Brother!" They kept their distance, considering him with caution, as they would a Frenchman—or an American.

They sat down and Ahmed ordered the *couscous*. The

waiter brought a huge platter of steaming semoula and mutton, over which he poured a red sauce filled with vegetables and hot pepper. Simeon had never tasted the Arab dish before. It stung his tongue, like hot barbecue on South Street or Lenox Avenue. He looked around the café. Nobody was paying any attention to him now. He felt more at ease.

Ahmed said, "Is it like this . . . the black neighborhoods in America?"

"Yeah." He thought a moment. "There is more laughter among the Negroes, though."

"They're not at war. Not the shooting kind."

"No."

Ahmed did not look like the other Algerians. He was better dressed and gayer, more expansive than the other Algerians in the restaurant.

"Your family's well off?" Simeon asked.

Ahmed flushed. "Yes. They're traders in Kabylia. I'm lucky, they send me money for school." He looked around the room. "Half of these men are out of jobs. The lucky ones who work are laborers; they dig ditches and do other things the French don't want to do. Cheap labor, about thirty thousand francs a month. What's that in dollars?"

"About sixty-five."

"And still, it's a lot more than they could make in Algeria. About a fifth of the Algerians at home live on the money these men send home."

Where was Maria? Simeon did not know why he thought of her suddenly or why he had not thought of her before. Probably at Enghein, with her "Paris mother," gambling at the casino. Another world.

"It must be hard, without women," Simeon said.

Ahmed nodded. "The women stay home. They'd be an

expense here. You probably wonder what the men do for women?"

"Yes."

"Most of the time, they do without. Sometimes, on payday, they go to a prostitute, if she'll have them. Most Frenchwomen won't go out with Algerians. A few with strong characters will, but they are the minority."

Simeon remembered that he had never seen an Algerian with a Frenchwoman. You could not walk down a street on the Left Bank without running across mixed couples, black and white, but the black people here, Africans or West Indians or Americans, were not laborers and were rarely poor. They were students, artists, professional people. They were "respectable."

Simeon felt uneasy; life had become too soft for him in Paris. That afternoon he had finished the last of a series of six absurd articles on the love lives of the Impressionists and mailed them off to *He-Man* magazine. But although the articles were ridiculous Simeon had had a feeling of accomplishment simply because he had done *something*. The plague of the foreign colony was idleness. A check would be mailed off to him in a week or so. He could pay for his apartment, lounge in cafés, go to the theater or to good restaurants when he wanted to. He looked around him, and thought of Hossein, the Algerian who had called him "white man."

He said, "I'd like to see Hossein again."

Ahmed smiled. "I told him we might drop by. He lives near here."

"And the man I had the fight with?" He felt embarrassed again, mentioning it.

"He's disappeared."

"Disappeared?"

"You sound surprised. It happens every day. More often in Algeria than here, but here in France also. He was probably picked up in a raid and sent to a concentration camp."

Simeon was stunned by the idea, and by the casualness with which Ahmed had said it. "You're not serious. There are concentration camps in France?"

Ahmed looked surprised now. "You didn't know? Even the newspapers talk about them. They're called 'internment camps,' but the difference lies mainly in the word. There are two right near Paris, and the others are in the Midwest and South. I thought everybody knew. Algerians disappear every day, and later you learn they're in such-and-such a camp. They're not so agreeable, these camps. No gas chambers, of course, but the guards and officials are not gentle. It's worse in Algeria. There torture has been developed into a high art. Shall we finish the coffee and go to Hossein's room?"

3

The rooming house where Hossein lived had narrow shadowy hallways, and the splotched plaster walls were so damp and filthy that Simeon shrank from them as he climbed the stairs. The musty air was filled with the melancholy Arab music and the smell of cooked food. All the doors were ajar and you could see groups of Algerians talking softly, on chairs or beds, under bare electric bulbs. Hossein lived on the fifth floor. His room was small, with a stark bulb hanging from the ceiling; the wallpaper was torn and stained, a worn linoleum was on the floor. There was no mattress or sheet on the narrow bed; a spare blanket, serving as mattress, was stretched across the springs. Simeon was sure there were bedbugs and perhaps fleas. The smell of the food which had been cooked on the alcohol burner under the washstand was stifling.

Hossein grinned and shook Simeon's hand. "Welcome to paradise. How does the white man feel?"

Simeon smiled. "The white man feels all right."

Ahmed and Simeon sat on two shaky chairs while Hossein heated a pot of coffee on the burner. Simeon looked around the room. There was a lopsided table, a closet and a suitcase. The washstand was partly torn from the wall. He would not like to live here, he thought, but he had seen even worse rooms on South Street.

Ahmed said, "This is only *partly* Hossein's room. He has it for eight hours a day. Two other men have it also for eight hours each. They sleep in rotation. That way, they split the rent three ways. None of them could afford to pay the rent alone.

Simeon got up and went to the window. It was getting dark, now. Under the street lamps he saw the idle men and the passing cops with their submachine guns. This was the Goutte d'Or quarter of Paris, Ahmed had told him. "Drop of Gold." He smiled sardonically.

"Do Algerians have to live in certain quarters?" he asked, turning.

Ahmed shrugged. "There's no law, if that's what you mean. We just run into: 'Sorry, no rooms; sorry, we're all filled up.' Know what I mean?"

"Oh, yes. I know."

Hossein put two cracked cups on the table. "Education of the white man," he said, glancing at Simeon. But now there was no hostility in his teasing. As he poured the coffee he said, "Sorry there's no cognac or wine. I was broke. Besides, Moslems aren't supposed to drink."

They drank the coffee in silence. Simeon looked at the two men. Their skins were white, all right: they looked like Southern Slavs. The way Hossein jokingly called him "white man" was ridiculous, he thought—as though he, Hossein, were not white! One of the Brazilians had explained to Simeon that in South America when an Indian or a Negro became rich or became a general, he was officially considered white. It was crazy. The world was a pyramid, and at the apex were the great rich peoples—the Northern Europeans, the English and recently the Americans. They imposed their sliding scale on the rest of the world. Here, the black man was inferior; there the Arab, there the Jew, there the Asiatic—according to where you were. And the people who became rich and great through historical accident were those who ruled. For that particular time.

Hossein said, "Well, what do you think of our castle?"

"Reminds me of slum tenements in Harlem or Philadelphia."

Hossein nodded. He looked at Simeon intently and said, "The Negroes in America should revolt, like we did."

Simeon said, "We don't have any Algeria to free."

"You have a country. Africa."

It was hard to explain. Africa was far away, in time as well as miles, and most American Negroes, while enthusiastic about the independence movement in Africa, would feel and be treated like complete foreigners there. The American Negro had, because of a specific experience, become something specific—neither African nor typically American. Things could change, things were evolving, and perhaps some day—

He finally said, "A lot of Negroes will go to Africa. But not all. You can't make it a revolutionary program."

"And you?"

"I don't know where I'm going."

"What do you feel like, living here, a black man in a white country?"

"Like a man without a country. Like the wandering Jew."

"That can't go on forever."

Simeon shrugged. "I didn't wish it. It's not on me that it depends."

There was a loud rapid knocking, the door sprang open, and an excited Algerian rushed in. "Hossein!" He spurted something in Arabic and ran out again, closing the door behind him. There were frantic running footsteps in the hall. Simeon looked at Ahmed questioningly, alarmed. Hossein jumped up and began shoving papers under a false bottom in the closet drawer. Ahmed said to Simeon, "Police raid. Have you got your passport?" "Yes." They heard heavy footsteps mounting the stairs, then loud knocks on doors followed by the imperious word *Police*! The knock rang on their door. Hossein opened it calmly.

An inspector in civilian clothes showed his badge. Behind him stood a policeman with a submachine gun. The inspector entered, and the cop stood in the doorway, his finger near the trigger of the gun.

"Papers," the inspector said. The policeman looked at them a moment and, as the inspector looked at their papers, began searching through the closets and drawers.

The inspector looked at Simeon, squinching his eyes. "You're not an Arab."

"No."

"Let me see your papers." Simeon showed his passport. The inspector said, "What are you doing here?"

"Visiting a friend."

The inspector looked at him suspiciously. He beckoned to the policeman, who approached and patted Simeon under the arms and at the hips to make sure that he was not carrying a weapon.

"You work for the FLN?" the inspector asked, studying Simeon's face with a frown.

"No," Simeon said, remembering that FLN were the initials of the Algerian National Liberation Front.

The inspector continued to study his face. "You're a foreigner. I wouldn't advise you to get mixed up in our internal affairs; understand what I mean? You could be expelled from the country at the slightest suspicion. Understand?"

"Yes."

"Stick among the foreigners. You've got nice cafés over there on the Left Bank. Stay out of trouble. All right?"

"Yes."

The inspector beckoned to the policeman and, with a final glance over their shoulders at Simeon, they left.

More police were in other rooms. Through the paper-thin walls, you could hear them asking sharp questions or opening drawers. The entire house seemed alive. Simeon could almost hear it humming. Hossein winked at Simeon with a smile. Ahmed went to the window.

"They've got an army down there," he said. He turned to Simeon. "I'm sorry. I don't want to get you in trouble."

"I'm glad I'm here. I feel . . . baptized."

Hossein grinned. "That's the spirit."

Later, through the window, they saw the police loading a score or so of Algerians into the patrol wagons outside.

"Off to the concentration camps," Ahmed said.

"Or worse," Hossein said.

"What do you mean by worse?" Simeon asked.

"Beating. Torture, maybe. To get information about the FLN."

Ahmed and Simeon did not stay much longer. At the door, Hossein grinned, and shook Simeon's hand. "You're not so bad for a white man," he said. On their way to the bus stop the police stopped Ahmed and Simeon twice and each time asked to see their papers.

III

I

"Come on by for dinner tonight," Babe had told the boys. "Leroy Haines just taught me how to make some of that fine barbecued chicken he fixes up at his restaurant in Pigalle. It'll sting the tongue."

Babe was a race man. He enjoyed nothing better than sitting in his comfortable apartment chatting and joking with members of the Negro colony in Paris. His place was cozy, with a fireplace which roared in winter, soft armchairs, good records and always plenty to eat and drink. He was a born host; you could drop in to see him at any time and he'd make you feel welcome.

Babe went into the kitchen to get dinner while, in the living room, gossiping and joking, sat Simeon and Maria, Benson, Doug, Harold, and an assortment of women: two English girls, Pat and Pamela; a French painter named Claire, Babe's Swedish girl friend Marika, and the two Negro blues singers, Mathilda and Gertie. All were drinking Pernod or red wine.

Mathilda, a lean hoarse blues singer who had once been with Count Basie's band, was looking at Doug and shaking her head.

"Listen everybody," she said, "I got an announcement to make. Our boy Doug here done got himself all mixed up in a love affair with an American heiress! My people are a bitch!"

She winked at Gertie, who was immense, with twinkling eyes and a hearty laugh. "A heiress, did you say? An *American* heiress? A *white* American heiress? You mean to tell me that our boy Doug here..." She looked at him, shaking her head in mock disbelief. "What's all this they saying about you, Doug? Thought you had a cute little French girl."

Doug grinned sheepishly. With his heavy Southern accent, he said, "Well, she ain't exactly a heiress, but she got a little money. Her father's a big man in the State Department."

"State Department!" Gertie's eyes became round as doughnuts. "Mathilda, did you hear what the man said?"

"I heard him! I heard him!"

Mouth open, Gertie looked around the room, then at Doug again. "Now, Doug, you listen to me, I'm one of the sisters and I got your interests at heart. You go on home to the States 'fore you get yourself in some *real* trouble. You hear me? Back to the States and get yourself a nice, simple little down-home girl from—where'd you say that place was you come from?"

"Tougaloo."

"Tougaloo!" Gertie doubled up with laughter. "Tougaloo where?"

"Tougaloo, Mississippi...."

"You hear him, you hear him?" Gertie shouted. "Hey, Babe, back there, you hear this man Doug here?"

Babe stuck his head around the door. "I heard him." He stared at Doug as though seeing a ghost. Doug grinned his sheepish grin, shifted his feet and, looking at the floor, said slowly in his Mississippi drawl, "Ain' nothing wrong with it over *here*."

Babe stared at Doug in horror. "Listen here, son," he said, "I'm gonna give you some advice. You better get your black behind back to Tougaloo where Senator Bilbo can keep an eye on you!"

Doug frowned. "Bilbo's dead."

"What's that!" Babe shouted.

"I said Bilbo's dead."

Babe's eyes rolled as though *he* were going to pass away. "Boy, did I hear you say *Bilbo*, just out plain like that, instead of saying, '*Mister* Bilbo, *sir*,' like your mammy taught you!" Babe stood in the doorway, his hands on his hips, then shook his head in despair and indignation and returned to the kitchen.

He returned carrying a platter of barbecued chicken and a bowl of greens.

"Okay, leap into it!" Babe said.

Benson looked amazed. "Babe, where in hell did you find greens in Paris?"

Babe chuckled. "A good race man finds green *any*where. Stink good, don't they? See the French grocers throw 'em away, so I made a deal with my own personal grocer." He cast a sly glance at Benson. "Made a deal with my butcher, too. He saves spare ribs for me. Dirt cheap."

Doug had stopped scowling and served the wine. "Ladies first. An old gallant custom among us Southern gentlemen."

Mathilda said, "This Southern gentleman's gentlewoman grandmammy washed Scarlet O'Hara's britches!"

They settled down to eat.

Babe leaned back, wiping his hands and mouth with a napkin, and said, "Them French is something. Met one of the boys the other day, just drove up to Paris from Rome bringing another man and two women with him. The cats didn't know the chicks so well, so when they stopped overnight in a French hotel they took two rooms, one for the girls and the other for them. The manager of the hotel bows and smiles, but he don't understand English very well, and when he carries the bags upstairs he puts one of the girls with my buddy and the other with the other guy. My friend says, 'Look, man, you made a little mistake there . . .' Before he can finish the manager apologizes, turns red and all, and rushes and changes the bags, switching things so my friend is with the *other* girl and vice versa. 'No, no,' says my boy, 'I'm stayin in the room with the man and the two girls are sleepin' together.' The manager draws himself up to his full height and says, 'Sir! We'll have none of *that* in *my* hotel!'"

Everybody laughed, except Doug. Babe winked at the others and then said, "Whatsamatter, Tougaloo, you miss the point?"

"No," Doug said, staring into the distance as if to formulate his thought. "However, I had always been led to believe that the French were rather *broad-minded* about homosexuality."

Laughter exploded again. Simeon glanced at Maria, to see if she were following the conversation. Her lips were parted in a smile, then she looked in Simeon's direction. It was crazy, the effect she had on him! She was reserved and secretive despite her age. Several times in bed he had whispered fiercely, "I love you!" trying in vain to force the same words from her lips. Once he had angrily complained about her reticence to commit herself in words and she had shrugged with nervous impatience. "Why ruin things by defining them?" she had said.

2

After salad and dessert there was coffee and cognac. Babe sucked on a cigar and said, "You know, that story got me to thinkin about the difference between the French and the Anglo-Saxons, 'specially the Americans, when it comes to sex. It's a bitch. My mind wandered over all kinds of historical reasons why the Anglo-Saxons are messed up. Cold, rainy weather, for one thing. Then, they was barbarians until rather late, until the Romans made up their minds to colonize them and civilize them. Then the early industrialization and all this crap about the raw materials, about colonizing. See, I know the historical reasons for lots of their troubles, including why they're racists. But I thought about that story, and I figured it out: one of the reasons for their state comes from their weird notions about sex."

The English girls looked at Babe with narrowed eyes, prepared to advance a defense. Maria smiled at Simeon; they had heard Babe philosophizing before. Benson pinched his nose, his face expectant—he loved any talk against white people.

"It's that Puritanism," Babe said. "What kinda damn people can you produce when you bring 'em up to believe that the most natural function in the world is dirty and sinful? *Think* about it! If you teach this to kids, if that's the feeling in the air around them, you can't expect them to get rid of it just because a preacher mumbles a few words and they reply 'I do' one fine day. If it's dirty and sinful before marriage, then it's dirty and sinful after marriage. You're supposed to marry the Virgin and sleep with the Bitch. It's a mess, man, a mess.

"Now, you take their attitude toward Negroes. I know

the race problem don't come from sex, but sex has become a part of it. Because the white Americans, most of them, know deep down that their relations with their wives ain't all they should be, and they know the wives are dissatisfied, and they feel deep down that maybe the women long for something else. Now, the white man don't have to worry about most other white men, because they got the same upbringing and problems as him. But them black niggers! Walkin around with them loose-jointed hips, and dancin all them sexy dances! Liking good food and liquor and laughter—all them nasty *sensual* things! Them niggers is *dangerous*!"

Babe mused, puffing on the cigar. He was enjoying himself, and Benson watched and listened approvingly. Maria was lost in her private world; the English girls were amused.

"The white man don't think this *consciously*," Babe went on. "That would hurt his pride as a member of the master race. What he thinks in his head and what he says out loud is, 'I'm gonna protect my pure lily-white delicate virgin wife and all lily-white virgin American wives from them slobbering, filthy, smelly, rapacious, satanic *beasts*!' But what he really fears deep, deep down inside is, 'Maybe my lily-white delicate virgin wife and other lily-white delicate virgin women would like to take down their hair for once and throw their legs in the air and holler and scream in ecstasy with *them*!' Then he panics, man. All kinds of aggressiveness and rage inside. Attack any Negro he sees with a white woman on the street. That white woman is his *wife*!"

"Tell 'em 'bout it, Babe!" Benson said. He held his hand across the table. "Gimme some skin, man. You right!"

Simeon laughed. "And the French, Babe? What about them?"

"Hell, the Frenchmen ain't scared of no black men because

they ain't Puritans and they like screwin' themselves. They don't believe in no myth about us being the great lovers, because they believe in their *own* myth about Frenchmen being great lovers. A Frenchman feels he's as good as anybody and better than most in bed. He thinks that, black or white, it's all the same between the sheets. I knew a German chick when I was in the Army after the war, and she told me a white American officer had said to her: 'If you ever sleep with a black man, you'll never be satisfied again with a white man.' Hell, no Frenchman would ever be fool enough to say or think a thing like that. He'd be insulted if anybody said it to him; he'd never believe it. And he's right!"

Benson savored the cognac, his pale eyes narrowed and hazy from drinking. Simeon thought again what a tragedy it was that he had stopped writing; the man was very quiet, but it was evident that he had a lot to say.

"Nigger," Benson said softly, almost to himself, rolling the word like an olive on his tongue. "Along the lines of what you just said, Babe, I been thinking about Anglo-Saxon foreign policy and I got it figured out. It's based on the nigger view of history."

He spoke softly, and his face had taken on a dreamy abstracted quality. "See," he said, "them folks in the State Department and the Foreign Office think Castro is a nigger. They think Khrushchev is a nigger, 'cause he ain't Anglo-Saxon. They think the Chinese and Japanese are niggers. They even think the French and Italians and Spaniards are niggers. They think everybody's a nigger if he ain't white gentile American or English or German or maybe Scandinavian or Canadian. So when they have a big international conference or something, and Khrushchev gets mad and pounds his fist on the table, they look at each other in complete and sincere amazement and say, 'Now, what do you figure's got into that nigger? Don't he realize he's talkin to *white* folks?' That's how come they look so baffled and hurt all the time. They just don't understand."

Gertie bent forward, weeping with laughter. "Yah, yah, them people is all messed up. They sick puppies."

"Yeah, they're all messed up, all right," Babe concurred, getting up and beginning to clear the table. "That's why I'm over here away from 'em. And it's why I ain't never gonna go back. Wild horses couldn't drag me."

Simeon said, "And you, Benson? Are you going back?"

"Yeah," Benson said, "when they elect a black president."

Simeon helped Babe carry out the dishes. There was something he had wanted to say when everyone was talking, but in not wanting to break the mood he had held it back. But in the kitchen he blurted it out.

"Babe, have you met any Algerians since you've been here?"

Babe stiffened. He knew what Simeon was going to say. Then with a kind of defiance and without looking at Simeon he said casually, "Not many. Why?"

"I met some. We talked, I went out to the Algerian neighborhood." Simeon hesitated. He still did not want to disturb the mood. But he had to say it: "Seems to me that the Algerians are the niggers of France."

Babe flicked the tap impatiently; he was making another pot of coffee. It was obvious to Simeon that Babe had already thought a great deal about what Simeon was saying, and that he did not want to think about it any more.

"It's . . . different," he said softly, looking at Simeon. There was an expression of entreaty on his face. "There's a war on. The French and the Algerians are fighting; they're killing each other. It's not the same thing."

Simeon said: "What I saw up in the North of Paris wasn't different, Babe, war or not. The ghetto, the cops, the contempt—the same thing. And it was like that *before* the war—for a century. It was that that *caused* the war."

Babe snatched up the coffee pot. He spoke aggressively. "Forget it, man. Algerians are white people. They feel like white people when they're with Negroes, don't make no mistake about it. A black man's got enough trouble in the world without going about defending white people."

But he was not convincing, even to himself. He too, wanted to hold onto the new peace, the new contentment. Babe shifted his eyes from Simeon, and without saying any more, turned and went back to the living room. Simeon stayed in the kitchen alone for a minute, then followed him.

IV

"SURE you don't mind?" Hossein asked.

"Of course not. Why should I mind?" Simeon answered. But he felt uneasy as he unlocked the door of the Chateau Club. Simeon was now a member of the private night club that Babe had first taken him to, the club where the manager had thrown out the loud American tourists.

Simeon had been out walking with the four Algerians, Ahmed and Hossein and two of their friends, Ben Youssef and Mohammed, and as they neared the Boulevard Saint-Germain had said, "I have to leave you, now. Work calls. Got to meet a French dancer at the Chateau Club, get some photographs for a magazine."

"Chateau Club? What's that?" Hossein asked.

"A little place with candles where they play records and people dance."

"Dancers are always late, it's a law of the trade. What do you say? We'll go by with you and keep you company until she comes."

"Great."

To his own astonishment, Simeon felt uneasy. Why was that? Most of the people who went to the Chateau were ridiculous snobs, but Simeon liked being a member simply to show that he *could* be one for once in his life; it was the kind of exclusive club that would never have admitted him in the United States. Why hadn't he ever invited Ahmed and Hossein to the club before? Why had it always happened that he met them or had dinner with them only at the Tournon or at the Place de la Contrescarpe or in the Arab quarter, but had never even *thought* of inviting them to some of the de luxe restaurants and cafés? Was it that, considering the misery of the Algerians, he was ashamed to let them know about this frivolous side of himself? Or was it something worse?

Jean-Claude, the club manager, glanced questioningly at Simeon as he entered with the Algerians. There was the usual smoke, loud music and couples dancing in candlelight. Did coolness fall on the room as Simeon and the others came in? Robert, a waiter who usually greeted Simeon with a smile, bowed stiffly and waited until Simeon said, "A table, please," before leading them to a table in a far corner.

Simeon noticed the waiter's manner and felt he was back in Philadelphia. He glanced around the room and saw that the dancer was not there. Hossein had been right. The waiter stood erect and impersonal as a soldier, waiting for them to order. Coffee, the Algerians said. There was no coffee. Vichy mineral water, then. Simeon ordered gin and tonic.

"Happy, that waiter," Hossein said. He grinned, but he was nervous; so were Ben Youssef and Mohammed. From the door, Jean-Claude watched them warily. The Frenchmen and women at nearby tables turned to stare at them; there were whispers and laughs.

Simeon felt his face burn. But why should he care what these imbeciles were whispering among themselves! Racist bastards! But he was afraid of something. Of losing something. Acceptance, perhaps. The word made him wince. Of feeling humiliation again. For one horrible instant he found himself *withdrawing* from the Algerians—the pariahs, the untouchables! He, for the frightening second, had rejected *identification* with them! Not me! Not me! Can't you see, I'm *different*! the lowest part of himself had cried.

He looked down with shame.

"What're they staring at," he heard Hossein whisper angrily.

"Let 'em stare!" Ahmed said.

How could this be? Simeon thought. Escape—that was what he had wanted. Sitting here with the Algerians he was a nigger again to the eyes that stared. A nigger to the outside eyes—that was what his emotions had fled.

The door opened and the dancer he had been waiting for came in. She spoke to Jean-Claude, who pointed to Simeon. She beckoned to Simeon, and pointed toward the bar.

"There's the dancer. I'll be right back," Simeon said.

Ahmed said, "We were just keeping you company. We'll take off, now."

"No, stay," Simeon said, almost sharply.

Ahmed hesitated. Hossein looked at Simeon with a smile. "Okay, we'll wait for you."

"It won't take long."

He joined the dancer at the bar. "Hello," she said. "The light is better here. Strange company you keep." She carried an envelope with the photographs.

Simeon said, "What's strange about them?"

"Why, those were *bicots*."

She said it with the naïve candor of a white American saying, "Why, those are niggers, my dear, you couldn't really…"

Simeon felt like hitting her. "Those *bicots* are giving your pure Aryan army a hard time, aren't they! Those are friends of mine. I don't know you. Let's stick to business."

She whistled softly. "Okay, okay, don't chop my head off. Let's get finished with the interview, shall we? By the way, I'll have a Scotch."

When Simeon returned to the table about twenty minutes later, he found Hossein flushed with anger, Ben Youssef and Mohammed frozen into pale masks. Ahmed seemed more natural, but very tense.

"They'd do better just not to let us into the place!" Hossein hissed. "That would be honest at least. But, no! They bow hypocritically and let you in and serve you, and everybody stares and gets all icy and whispers. I hate 'em! I hate the French! With their slick manners and twisted hearts!"

Ahmed tried to calm him. At a nearby table, people laughed. Hossein's eyes shot up, defiant; he was certain that they were laughing at *them*. But a calm now settled over Simeon. The bad moment had passed. He had crossed the bridge, and felt at one with the Algerians. He felt strangely *free*—the wheel had turned full circle.

Suddenly, in the quiet of the room, Ben Youssef began talking rapidly and loudly in Arabic. His words tumbled out, and Simeon sensed that he was speaking almost uncontrollably simply to break through the icy atmosphere. Perspiration streamed down his face, and as his voice rose almost hysterically the voices of the other people in the club died down and a hush came over the room. People stared. Ben Youssef talked on and on; something had snapped inside him and he could not stop himself. Mohammed looked at him wide-eyed, nodding stiffly now and again. Hossein and Ahmed seemed hypnotized as they watched Ben Youssef with strained expressions. Simeon's muscles tightened and his hands trembled. He felt a terrible sorrow for Ben Youssef, wanted to calm him, to help him, to take him by the hand

and lead him out, lead him to safety. But none of them could move.

All tension suddenly exploded. Ben Youssef laughed loudly, his eyes bulging, perspiration standing out in beads on his forehead. The others laughed loudly, too, shouting agreement to what Ben Youssef was saying. Simeon was sure he was saying nothing, he was saying words. But he too found himself laughing.

The room was silent, now, except for the music. No one danced, everybody stared at the four *bicots* and the nigger, thinking they had gone crazy. Ben Youssef's face was eerie in the candlelight. Jean-Claude, the manager, came out from the barroom and stood in the doorway looking with distaste at the group.

Then, a woman's voice could be heard addressing itself to a companion: "Really, they let just *anybody* in the Chateau these days, it seems."

Ben Youssef leaped to his feet. He stood livid, his lip trembling, staring at the woman who had spoken. The woman, a beautiful blonde of about thirty, smiled faintly in amusement and glanced at her companion. Her escort smiled also, looking at the waiters and at Jean-Claude for reassurance.

"You talking about us?" Ben Youssef said, stuttering in his heavily accented French.

Simeon shared Ben Youssef's fury, but was anxious that he do nothing rash—the police would ask no questions.

The woman said smiling, "Cher Monsieur, I don't believe we've been introduced."

She let out a shriek as Ben Youssef moved toward her, grinning. "Don't yell. Don't be scared. Ain't gonna hurt you. Just wanta dance with you. How's that? You dancing with a *bicot*, be nice for that perfumed body of yours, huh? C'mon. Stand up! We're gonna dance!"

The woman gasped as though she were going to faint. Her companion looked at Ben Youssef indignantly. "This young lady..." he began.

"Now, you keep out of this," Ben Youssef said, pointing a threatening finger at him. "All of you keep out of this. I'm in a mood to tear me a Frenchman to pieces tonight." He grinned again. "This is between me and the lady, ain't it Mademoiselle? Come on, now. Let's dance."

He moved to take her hand, and she screamed. The manager, followed closely by the waiters, rushed over and took Ben Youssef by the shoulder. Ben Youssef whirled, striking Jean-Claude's hand.

"Take your dirty French hands off me!"

"Get out of here! You and your friends!"

"*Put* me out if you're big enough!"

"I'll call the police."

"Call them! I'm ready for some police tonight!"

Enraged, the manager turned toward Simeon. "You brought these people in here. Get them out. I'm not joking, I'll call the police."

Simeon opened his mouth to say something, but Ahmed stood up and said, "Let's go. To hell with them."

"I ain't going nowhere," Ben Youssef said. "I'm beginning to enjoy myself here."

Hossein took Ben Youssef by the arm. "It's not worth it. We see enough cops every day."

Ben Youssef and Hossein argued in Arabic. Finally, Ben Youssef calmed down, and let Hossein and Ahmed lead him toward the door. There was a loud buzz of voices in the room as they left.

Simeon threw the money for the drinks on the table. The manager picked it up and shoved it back into Simeon's hand.

"Never mind the money. Keep it. Just return your key. We don't want you back here . . . you and your friends."

Simeon tossed the money and the key back on the table. "You couldn't drag me back here," he said.

Outside, Ben Youssef was still furious and he argued with the others in Arabic. Ahmed tried to calm him.

Hossein said to Simeon, "You regret losing your key?"

"Oh, no!"

"You sure? I knew what the Chateau was when I suggested we stop by with you. I was surprised when you agreed. Life gets complicated sometimes. I know how you felt. You don't regret anything?"

"You sonofabitch," Simeon laughed. "Was that a test? Did I pass?"

"You did okay," Hossein said. He winked and put a hand on Simeon's shoulder.

V

I

THE WEATHER had suddenly turned much cooler; the sun had disappeared, and a thick gray haze hovered over the rooftops. Passing the Monaco Café, Simeon saw Clyde just inside the window, leaning on a table with seven cognac saucers in front of him. Joey the Drunk stood at the bar, staring sullenly toward the street. It was late afternoon and Maria had not yet returned from her acting class, so Simeon went to Le Village for a quiet drink while he read *Le Monde*. In one of the cushioned alcoves he saw Jinx, Clyde's wife, sitting with her six-year-old daughter and a strange man.

Simeon resigned himself to the fact that he would have to speak to them. That child was going to become alcoholic just from the fumes, and a nymphomaniac by proximity. Jinx saw him and called, "Hey, Simeon, how are you? Come on over and meet Jacques."

Simeon shrugged and walked over to Jinx's table.

"Hello."

"Have you seen Clyde? He been asking about me?" She was good-looking, Simeon thought, but her hysterical eyes were too close together; she shook that horse-tail of hair like a whip.

"I just saw him at the Monaco. Didn't talk to him."

"The drunken ass. He'll probably be in a foul mood as usual and take another swing at me when I get home tonight. *If* I get home." She smiled at Jacques, a Frenchman apparently versed in the odd ways of American women tourists. "Join us, Simeon. Have a drink."

"I have to run. I'm just finishing one at the bar."

"You're always running when you see me."

2

Simeon went to the Tournon, where he knew Maria would look for him. The café was noisy and convivial; he waved to Madame Alazard, the owner, and to the old men playing bridge and belote. In the rear he found Ahmed with Henri, and at an adjoining table Lou playing chess with his girl friend Betty. He ordered a beer.

Henri was saying, "I just wanted you to know it. We're not all torturers and colonialists. Lots of us are against this war, especially the students."

"I know," Ahmed said. "I'm a student myself, I know. But you're not doing much."

"We have demonstrations..."

"That's not enough. You should refuse to serve in the Army."

"That would be...difficult."

"Everything's difficult."

Lou put in, "And of course, I suppose there's always the possibility of working with the FLN."

Ahmed smiled. "I wouldn't have dared to suggest it."

Simeon thought of Jinx. It always depressed him, seeing

her or Clyde or some of the other foreigners here. They epitomized how empty the lives of the expatriates could be.

Simeon thought of the recent scene at the Chateau Club. What was he doing here in Paris? What was he doing that made him any more worthwhile than Jinx?

3

But, God knew, he loved Paris. He loved simple things like being up all night, and in the morning going down to the Vert Galant, that green tip of the Île de la Cité that jutted into the Seine, and waving to the pilots of the barges.

He liked the faces of the ordinary French people—not the shopkeepers, not the politicians, not the intellectuals, not the officials or the police, but the bus drivers, the street cleaners, the news vendors, the workers at Les Halles, the trainmen, the bricklayers and carpenters and factory workers. He read into their eyes dim memories of the French Revolution, the Commune, the Resistance. These things were not forgotten, they were there still in the French people and through them in Simeon. These same eyes expressed humor and the sheer joy of life. These people were idealistic enough to believe in the future, but cynical enough to be wary of politicians and promised words on paper. Paris was all right.

He loved the "characters." Like the Paris joker who dragged an empty leash around Saint-Germain-des-Prés, and when you asked him "What are you doing?" replied, "I'm looking for the Invisible Man." "Why?" "I've found his dog."

Or Joey the Drunk, who had lived in a Red workers' district of Paris at the time of the "Americans-Go-Home" campaign and the "Ridgeway Riots," when Americans were insulted on the streets and American cars were spat on or worse. Joey had waked one morning to find *Yankee Go Home* painted in huge letters on his sidewalk. So he had gone out immediately and bought ten pounds of candy and an equal amount of spareribs, then walked through the neighborhood giving candy to every child he saw and a barbecued sparerib to each adult. That had worked. Nobody had suggested that he go home again.

With an automobile on a warm summer day you could drive out of the city and visit the Champagne and Burgundy regions and go down into the winecellars where they gave you free samples of the best wines. You didn't have to worry about whether the hotels would accept black people. You just drove through the beautiful countryside, stopping off in villages whenever you felt like it to eat or have a drink, and taking a hotel or boardinghouse room wherever you happened to be in the evening.

But he could not help thinking about race in Paris or anywhere. How can you help thinking about the thing that dominates your life? So Simeon thought about race, thought of all those French mothers (and mothers-in-law) who walked through the streets of Paris proudly wheeling their brown babies. Or the night when he had been at a night club and a French Negro woman who had been drinking too much stood up tall and beautiful and danced sensuously alone by candlelight, drawing admiring stares and applause, and the jealous blond French actress who commented within earshot of Simeon: "Hmmmph! She thinks she's better than anybody else just because her skin is black!"

Things were different from the States all right. The night that he had walked with the Brazilians to the Arch of Triumph, they had held their arms outstretched over the eternal flame and he and the others had joined Carlos in this vow: "We'll never leave this beautiful city. If anybody tries to make us leave, we'll chain ourselves to the lampposts!"

Ahmed had explained: "It goes like this. The police make a raid and pick up every Algerian in sight. They take you to the station, and if you don't have a record they mark your name on a card and let you go. A short time afterwards, they make another raid and pick up everybody in sight, you included. They check the records and see your name on the card and say, 'Aha! A troublemaker. You've already been arrested once, you're a second offender.' So they send you to jail for a week or so, and then they let you go free with a warning. So you're sitting in a café, drinking a coffee or something, and the police burst in; it's a raid, everybody in the wagon. 'The third time!' the sergeant exclaims, and this time you go to jail for a longer stretch. Maybe you're beaten first, to make you give information about the FLN. Sometimes the beating is done with clubs, sometimes with rubber hoses. Can you imagine how this feels?"

"Yes, I can imagine."

"Maybe finally you're released again. They make another raid and you're picked up and you disappear. Nobody ever hears from you again. God knows what's happened to you. And you've never done a thing, not a thing!"

4

As Henri left the café, Ahmed's eyes followed the student out of the door.

"He's a nice person," Ahmed said to Simeon and Lou. "He's got a conscience, and is tormented by what's happening to the Algerians. That's more than you can say for most Frenchmen."

"Don't you think most of the French are tormented?" Lou asked.

"Not tormented. They've got bad conscience, but they react by just not thinking about it. Television, football, wage increases—that's all they want to think about."

"I've seen some demonstrations against the war. That took courage, because the police swung their clubs mighty hard against the demonstrators, cracking heads right and left."

"How many demonstrators? One thousand? Five thousand? Ten thousand? Twenty thousand? There are forty-five million Frenchmen! That's no way to stop a war. . . . But Henri's all right. He'll act on what he believes. People like him can keep Algerians from hating all Frenchmen."

Simeon and Lou began a game of chess while waiting for Maria. Lou was Simeon's favorite among the white Americans in Paris. He was reserved, but had a quiet intelligence and good sense of humor. His unobtrusive patriotism was rooted in what Simeon thought best in America's history and legend: the old pioneer spirit, the individualism, the belief in every man's equality with every other man, the vision of the United States as a melting pot of peoples and races. He realized that the reality did not come up to this vision, but held to the image as a goal.

Lou said, "When I was a kid, I lived in a mixed neighborhood, I grew up with Negro kids as well as white kids. Everything was fine until we started going to school. Then Negroes went to one school, and the white kids to another. That was a shock to me, my first real awakening to the color problem."

Simeon said, "Yeah. There must have been a lot of others afterward, though."

"And how! I keep thinking about one incident. When I was drafted, a Negro fellow I knew and I got on the train together to go to Fort Mead. We talked all the way to Maryland, sharing our sandwiches and discussing jazz, and when we got to Mead we got into line together to pick up our bedding for the night. We were having a great conversation, when all of a sudden a sergeant came out and shouted: 'All colored men step out of the line.' This friend of mine and I stared at each other in stupefaction. We had been talking and laughing and then suddenly somebody had smashed the draw-bridge between us. He looked at me with a faint smile—I had a funny feeling it was as though he were accusing *me*—and then stepped out of the line. They led all the colored fellows away to another part of the camp and kept them in segregated barracks. From time to time I ran across my friend, but he was cool. We would exchange a few embarrassed words, but things could never be the same again. The bridge was broken."

Simeon nodded. He had heard a dozen stories like this. Lou said, "It's a relief talking to you like this. This color and race problem obsesses me; it always did. I always wanted to get closer to Negroes, but it was hard, the Negroes themselves were suspicious of me. When I would go to Negro neighborhoods in the States, I had the feeling that the Negroes were rejecting *me*. Know what I mean? It's complicated. One day I was coming out of the subway in Harlem and a Negro walked up to me and without a word hauled off and punched me in the face. I fell, blood spurting all over, and the Negro calmly got on the subway and the train pulled off."

Simeon said sympathetically, "It's not that easy, Lou. The trouble is, nobody could read your mind. When people get classified into castes, they classify the dominant group, too. I had a friend who had a prejudiced white Southerner commanding officer while he was in the army. It was an all-Negro unit, and the officer took out all his racism on the soldiers, really giving them a hard time. This friend, Charlie, knew he had to take it while he was in the Army, but he told himself: 'Dammit, when I get out of this friggin' Army the first person who speaks to me with a Southern accent is gonna get knocked on his rear.'

"So he got discharged and sent home. When he was getting off the train in Pennsylvania Station a man walked up to him and smiled and said with a Southern accent, 'Pardon me, could you-all tell me where I can find——' He never finished that sentence. Charlie sighed, put down his bags and knocked that poor man flat on his back. It's sad, the poor Southerner was probably a nice guy. *He* might not even have been a racist. But any member of the privileged group in a racist society is considered guilty. Every white South African is guilty. Every Frenchmen is guilty in the eyes of the Algerians. Every white American is guilty. The guilt can end only when racism ends."

Lou stared wonderingly at Simeon. "Yeah. It's what I feel. Always guilty, even though *I'm* not racist. Crazy."

Hossein and Ben Youssef had come into the café and had listened silently to the conversation of the two Americans. Hossein seemed surprised to see Simeon talking to a white man from the United States.

A few minutes later, Maria hurried into the café, her eyes shining with excitement.

"I'm late," she said apologetically to Simeon. "I was shopping with Anushka, my Paris mother.... Darling, she took me shopping. I've got new *shoes*, Simeon. *Three* pairs. And two *beautiful* dresses, and a necklace and bracelet. She is *crazy* with money, Anushka!"

Breathless, Maria sat down and ordered a hot tea. Ben Youssef and Hossein were meeting her now for the first time, and they watched with curiosity as she opened her packages to show her treasures to Simeon.

Betty whistled when Maria unwrapped the bracelet, which appeared to be made of jade. Maria held it up and stared at it for a long moment, as though she could not believe it really belonged to her. "Is beautiful," she whispered. "Beautiful." I never had something so beautiful. But I am bit afraid. I am afraid I lose it. Paris mother is crazy, was so expensive, I did not want her to buy it. But it could not cost so much. I am sure we were cheated."

Ben Youssef smiled. His face, too, was boyish, like Ahmed's, and he seemed all innocence as he casually and unwittingly dropped his bomb: "Sure," he said, "probably some dirty Jew sold it to you."

The words exploded full in their faces. Maria jerked her head up as though she had been slapped. Lou's mouth dropped slightly open, Betty's eyes widened in surprise and pain. Hossein seemed to notice nothing, but Ahmed nervously looked from Simeon to Maria. Simeon was stunned. Those words, from one of the *Algerians*? Abruptly a whole mental and psychological structure he had built up since the day he had first talked with Hossein seemed to collapse.

Maria's face was white with anger; all frivolity had gone. "I am dirty Jew," she said.

Ben Youssef became pale and tried to smile, but couldn't. "Just a word," he said. "It slipped out. I'm sorry."

Maria said, "No reason to be sorry. You said what you thought."

"It's a word; just like that it came to my tongue, I wasn't thinking. I didn't mean it."

Lou coughed nervously. Hossein looked around the table, particularly at Maria, he seemed still unperturbed. Simeon thought was *everybody* a racist toward somebody else, then? He had never given much thought to prejudice against Jews, he had been too much personally involved in the question of color.

"It's the war," Ahmed said hesitantly. "The war between Israel and the Arabs. It provoked reactions. You must forgive Ben Youssef."

"Is not just the war," Maria replied with quiet intensity, staring straight ahead as though concentrating on something. "This existed before the war, and you cannot even call it anti-Semitism, because Arabs are Semites, too. It is crazy." Her face seemed both tired and defiant as she swept them with the eyes behind the dark glasses. It was a visible effort for her to speak about a subject she did not like to discuss. "For thousands of years this has gone on. Why? In Poland there were pogroms. The Germans burned us in ovens. People hate us in North Africa, in Middle East, in Europe, in America, everywhere? Why? What do we do to anyone, tell me that. Poland now is Communist and is supposed to stand for equality for all, and still it is horrible to be a Jew there. You cannot get certain jobs, there is hatred and persecution. You are spat on in streets. Why?"

She looked at Hossein, held her eyes steady on his. "You say nothing, but I see it in your eyes. You hate Jews."

Hossein said with sudden passion, "Worse than I hate the French! Worse than I hate the colonialists!"

Simeon winced. In that moment he detested Hossein. Ahmed was distressed.

Maria was cold and calm. "Why?"

"Because they are Semites. Because they are like us and should be with us, on our side, but consider themselves different, consider themselves better, and place themselves on the side of the colonialists against us. I hate them because of Israel, because they took Arab territory and drove the Arabs out. I can tell you about North Africa and the Jews! Who was the spy in our midst for the French? The Jews! Who made profits on our backs? The Jews! When we felt that weight on our backs, when we looked up to see who was on our backs, who did we see just above, on our backs, smiling and weighing hard? The Jews! Don't talk to me about the Jews. I can tell you about the Jews!"

Maria bit her lip. Simeon said, "You're raving, Hossein. The Jews are persecuted as much as we are."

"Then they should be on our side! What are they doing on our backs? Hated by the colonialists, but still despising *us!* Playing both ends against the middle!"

Lou intervened, speaking gently because he was the only "pure" white person there. "Every oppressed group is oppressed in a different way and has a different history," he said. "The history of the American Negro is not the same as the history of the colonized African or Asian. The end products are different, too. The history of the Jews in the Middle Ages led them to become tradesmen and moneylenders *to survive.* They were banned from practically all other professions, but Christians were forbidden to become moneylenders so at least the Jews could do that. Middlemen. It's true, they drifted through hostile societies, hated, rejected and persecuted, becoming middlemen for their own self-preservation. And naturally they adopted defensive attitudes. They were always threatened and they wanted to hold on, hold on to whatever security they had, and maybe that's part of the reason they sided with the French in North Africa."

Hossein said: "You can give any excuse you like. For me, they're on the side of the enemy, and that's all I need to know. I shoot!"

"I said *part* of the reason," Lou went on. "But the other part of the reason is that the Moslems themselves rejected them. The Moslems themselves refused to consider the Jews as one with them. The Jews in North Africa were torn between two things; I *understand* how you come to think the way you do, but you should try yourself to understand."

Hossein stood up. He was very calm, looked first at Lou, then at Simeon, then at Maria. He said to Maria, "I apologize. I apologize first because you're with Simeon, and he's a friend. Second, because you seem like a nice person and I'm sorry I offended you." To Simeon he said: "Excuse me. I know what you're thinking, but don't judge me wrong. I get carried away when I talk about things I really believe." He turned to Lou and said, "I understand nothing. You hear?—*nothing*. There are historical reasons for everything, even for the French occupation of Algeria, even for slavery, but I don't understand historical reasons. I just judge by end products. I accept the end products, I embrace the end products, or else I shoot the end products before they shoot me. I am a very simple man. I'm going home to bed, now. I'm not good at discussing. I get angry, and there's no point in that."

Ahmed said, "You should stay, Hossein."

"Yes, I know, intellectual, you like to hear words."

"You can't always run away from words. There'll come a day when the shooting will stop, and we'll have to use words instead."

"Not me. It's too late. There'll always be someplace where

people are talking with more than words, and I'll be there. On the right side."

Ben Youssef stood up, too. It was clear that he had been lost in the conversation, and frightened by the heat his casual words had generated. He wanted to be in the secure company of Hossein.

"I'm ... I'm very sorry," Ben Youssef said to Maria before leaving.

Maria did not look at him, nor did she reply.

VI

I

MUCH LATER that night Simeon and Maria walked towards Simeon's apartment. The street was dark and cold. Police paced back and forth in front of the Luxembourg Palace. Although they were near Simeon's apartment, Maria said, "I don't feel like going in yet. Let's walk. Maybe go the Caméléon." Simeon nodded, thinking of the incident with Hossein.

They did not talk, but Simeon felt very close to Maria and knew that she felt close to him. They passed in front of the Mephisto, waving to friends, then up the rue de Seine to the river before circling and turning back.

"I don't like to discuss such things," Maria said finally. "It twists me inside and makes me ill."

Simeon was silent. He had wanted to say more back in the café, when Hossein and the others were talking, but he had been angry and had not known what to say. How do you argue against a blind prejudice? He remembered that many Negroes disliked Jews. There was a reason for it: the Jews, discriminated against in the white society, were often left with the crumbs—the real estate and stores in the Negro neighborhoods. They were therefore the most visible exploiters of the American Negroes, and detested by many Negroes because of this. The same must be true in North Africa. But how could you explain this to Hossein? Besides, the prejudice of the oppressed was much different, morally, from the prejudice of the oppressor.

"It's the first time I heard you talk this way," he said.

She shrugged. "Yes, and maybe the last. I swore to myself I would drop this kind of subject. In the end, everybody still thinks what he thought at first."

"Still, you have to say it."

"Why? Why bother? The world is terrible, Simeon."

"Terrible and wonderful, sweetheart."

"No. Terrible. I am nervous about something in you. There is a reason why you hunt out your Algerian friends. It is because they are in a troubled situation. I have a feeling that you cannot simply accept happiness. You have a good life, a nice apartment, enough money, but you cannot accept it. Something bothers you inside, so you go and look for complications. I am afraid for you. For me, too."

He understood what she meant. What she did not understand was that he longed for peace, quiet and the gentle life as much as she did. At least, he felt he did. Maybe you couldn't be sure, he thought, as he pushed open the heavy door of the Caméléon.

It was a small nightspot near the Odéon, with a jazz band and dancing in the cellar and a café where they played modern jazz records upstairs. John Coltrane's saxophone greeted them. The smoky room was crowded with Africans, American Negroes and young French jazz fans. They waved to Slim, a Nigerian drummer sitting at the bar, and inched their way to a tiny table in the rear.

Maria settled herself on the upholstered bench, leaned her head back and immediately became absorbed in the music. On barstools, lighted by the dim orange lamps, black men moved their shoulders rhythmically in a stationary "twist" to the music.

Maria said, "This is what I like. Music, enjoying myself, with no problems." She smiled at him. "How do you feel, Simeon? About being here? About our life?"

"I like it. Feel a bit restless sometimes, though. I don't want to go back to the States, not yet at least, but I feel . . . idle here. Life is pleasant, but I'm not *doing* anything. Just sort of . . . watching the sands trickle out."

He exasperated her. "But what do you want to *do*?"

"I don't know." He shrugged helplessly. "Just not simply stand on the sidelines, watching life go by."

"Goes by anyway." Nervously she lit a cigarette. "Makes no sense. What kind of terrible world is this? I go crazy when I think of the labor camp and my parents and how the prisoners were and the gas chambers. It makes no sense, none of it. So I try not to think."

Simeon had asked himself metaphysical questions years ago, a child looking at the stars, but he knew now that there were questions you could not answer. He knew now that the infinite was ungraspable, that one had to circumscribe one's world and live within it and its values if one wanted to *live* at all. A child starving to death was simple and clear, you did not have to know the destiny of Man to know you should give it food.

"Maria." He hesitated at the edge of the question, afraid of it. "Tell me something. Do you love me?"

She laughed, teasing. "Must be careful with that word."

"I am careful."

"Do you love me?"

"I think so."

She would not look at him. She watched the Africans

dance with their shoulders. "I like to be with you all the time, with you and with nobody else. That's all I know."

It was the nearest she had ever come to saying she loved him. What was she so afraid of? It was as though she were terrified by words. He realized again that her hold on him was much stronger than his on her. She was whole and round, distant, independent of him. But *he* could no longer imagine existence in Paris without her. He would lose her, this dark whisp of smoke would vanish from his life. He felt sure of it.

He wanted to force her to live in the real world, and asked, "Would you marry... a Negro?"

"Without hesitation," she said, turning to look at him. "There is only one thing—that he must be content to live and love in peace. He must not go around seeking complications, seeking 'causes' and problems. You understand? He must be able to live a normal life."

"There is no 'normal' life."

"Yes. Yes, there is."

"You mean a nice, middle-class suburban life, in a cocoon, cut off from the rest of the world?"

"Cut off from the troubles of the world. Yes. Doesn't have to be middle-class, how you say. But yes, this is right."

"That kind of life might not be possible for a Negro if he thinks and feels."

"Would be possible if he tries. If he loved me, he would try."

"The Jews in Poland during the war—was it possible for them to lead a normal life?"

She hesitated. She was fighting him, but also fighting with herself, against some consciousness or some truth she did not want to recognize. She almost shouted, desperately: "Yes! It was possible if they fled. You fled, I fled, no? In Poland, I am not talking about those captured or killed. Nothing could be done about that and I would not complain if it was situation where nothing could be done. I talk about those with free will. Those who could have fled and did not. My parents could have fled, they saw friends who fled, but they did not because they did not want believe the world was so terrible as it is. When they realized, it was already too late!"

Simeon wanted to stroke Maria's brow and soothe her. He wanted to take her in his arms and rock her like a baby. But the words he spoke were necessary—he was defending himself, too:

"Perhaps the Negro who might want to marry you might not be able to flee. Not forever. Because of something inside..."

Maria looked at his face, at the patch and the eye. "He can flee. He will be able to flee. If he loves me and wants to."

"You're selfish, Maria."

"But no!" She looked at him in hurt surprise. "Perhaps I am selfish in other things, but I am not selfish about this, what I am talking about now. But a man who loved me and married me would want me to be sane. I know what I feel, and what I can bear, and I don't want go crazy. I'd rather be alone, anything, but not that."

2

Lovers were kissing in a doorway up the street from the Caméléon. Near the Boulevard Saint-Germain, five or six tramps were piled together sleeping on a grill over the subway to benefit from the warm air rising from below.

"You stay with me tonight?" Simeon asked.

"Yes."

Maria hummed a tune they had heard in the night club. Her mood had changed completely now, and she seemed gay.

"I want lots of music. We'll buy records?"

"Yes."

"And we give a party. You have nice apartment to have a party in. You agree?"

"Wonderful idea."

"We invite Babe and Doug and Lou and Betty. I like Lou, he's a good American, you heard how good he talked today? And the Brazilians and maybe some of my Polish friends, too."

They slipped quickly into bed. Maria said, "I am happy about something. A movie director, the friend of the woman who runs our acting school, came to see us rehearse. He said I had talent and maybe someday would have a small part for me in one of his films."

"Marvelous. Let's celebrate." Simeon jumped out of the bed and fetched a bottle of beer with two glasses. He filled the glasses and returned to the bed where Maria was staring pensively at the ceiling.

"Don't you want the beer?"

She shook her head. Her look troubled him. He climbed back into bed, putting the beer glasses on the night table.

"Simeon, I talked to doctors. They'll operate on my eyes in a couple of months. I'm afraid."

Simeon was afraid, too, but did not want to show it. "Try not to be nervous, baby. It'll be all right. It'll be successful and then you'll be free, you won't have to worry any more."

"Yes."

She smoked a cigarette, exhaling heavily. "You know what I think sometimes?"

"What?"

"I think I am three persons. I am the Maria now, waiting for the operation. I am the *potential* Maria, the Maria who has had operation and can see and has a whole bright future ahead. And I am *potential* Maria with operation that has failed, a Maria who is blind."

She thought about it, flicking her ash absently onto the floor.

"You know what I think sometimes? That it would be better if the operation failed. That is the Maria I like best of all. It is the only one of the three I like."

VII

I

SIMEON stared for a long time at the photograph in the Paris *Herald Tribune*. Little Rock? No, another Southern American town where a handful of black children were going to school through lines of soldiers and howling mobs. The pictured showed five black girls and boys walking with heads held high through a crowd of white adults whose faces were twisted by hatred. Because five children with black skins were for the first time going to sit side by side with white boys and girls in a formerly all-white school.

The soldiers sent by the government were armed, standing between the black children and the white parents, between the black children and violence, between the children and death.

Simeon felt like weeping. He studied the white faces. Yes, he knew them, recognized them: the faces of the stone souls. Could these people really exist? As he stared at the photograph, the old terrors and hatreds swept over him again.

If he had a gun and saw these faces he would shoot. There was no doubt about that. So nothing had changed in him. He was still the same.

His eyes rested on the face of one of the black girls. The universe was the face of the girl. The face did not betray the fear the body felt. And what did she know, that girl of ten or twelve years old? Mama had said: "You're gonna go to the white school tomorrow, Lulu Belle. Gonna be a lot of white folks around, and they gonna shout nasty things, but don't you mind. It's important. You can't understand yet, but it's important for black people. You hear me? And we behind you, Papa and me and all the black people in America. So you just walk straight. Don't mind what they shout. Just walk straight, and tell yourself they stupid, and remember we all right there with you, Papa and me and Aunt Jessie and Uncle Wig and all the colored folks in town and all the colored folks in the world."

He was sitting on the terrace of the Café Tournon. At a table nearby sat Doug, discussing something with Clyde and Jinx. Simeon paid no attention to them. He was not interested in them.

"God's on our side," Lulu Belle's mother said. "He ain't with them dirty white folks, screamin' hate from their hearts. You hear?"

"Yes, ma'am."

"You ain't scared, are you honey? We can't let 'em keep us down forever, you understand."

"Yes, ma'am."

"Are you scared?"

"No'm," she lied, almost choking from the pounding of her heart in her throat.

And she'd walked the next morning through purgatory. Not turning to look at them people shouting dirty things. Scared, but proud. Because Mama and Papa were there, someplace back there, even though she couldn't see them. And all of the black people in town were back there, paying attention to her. And some white men were there taking her picture, and that would be in the papers, and colored people all over the country, all over the world, would see it. Mama had said so. And they'd all be proud of her. Because she didn't show she was scared.

"Nigger bitch, you ain't gonna go to that school long!"

"Black bastard, we gonna kill you before the term is out!"

"Go back to your nanny's hangin' titties where you belong!"

She heard them. But they wasn't gonna know how hard her heart was beating! They wasn't gonna know she was scared! Because maybe she wasn't scared! Because she was mad, she didn't like them crazy people nohow, and why should she be scared anyway? She wasn't scared! She wasn't scared! Them people was scared of little ole *her*! 'Cause they was crazy! Sweet Jesus, they was crazy! How come Jesus made crazy people like them!

Just walking straight ahead, not scared, into the school.

2

People talked to Simeon, there on the terrace, and he listened with only half an ear.

Joey the Drunk, who came staggering by: "Been working on my novel."

"That so."

"It's gonna be a *bitch* of a novel. Nearly finished. Benson and Dick Wright and Chester Himes—they ain't the *only* novelists around here in the quarter. Gonna be a *bitch*."

This was the novel Joey had been working on for years. Benson had read parts of it and had been embarrassed to find the writing of an eight-year-old child. He had not known what to say.

"A *bitch* of a novel," Joey said. "Let you read it some day."

Doug, who left Clyde and came to sit next to Simeon: "Hell, ain't it, them school riots?"

"Yeah."

"Nothing but bad news in the papers these days. Been reading 'bout the Congo, fighting and all. What you s'pose is going on down there?"

"Belgians don't permit any Congolese to get an education, then pull out. What do you expect?"

"Yeah. Looks bad, though. Simeon, I been wantin' to talk to you. Listen, I got a sort of woman problem. I'm in the Embassy, and that means I'm a State Department employee, right? Well, there's this white American girl, this girl Babe and them calls a heiress, and she's got a sort of crush on me, see what I mean? Now, her father's a high State Department man, got a lot of money, and he knows about the girl and me, but he don't mind, he's a liberal, see? So what do you think?"

"What's the problem?"

"Well, see, the trouble is, I'm sorta in love with another girl, the sweet little French girl you seen me with a few times, remember? I feel like marrying the French girl, we get along fine, all soft and nice together; she understands me. The American girl don't understand me worth a damn."

"Okay, marry the French girl."

"Well, it ain't that simple. I mean, how do I know how long I'm gonna want to stay in France? But I want to make a career in the State Department, and, hell, the American girl's pa could help me. See what I mean? I know it sounds materialistic, but, hell, man, life is materialistic. You ever try to eat soul? I got to think of the future."

"Marry the American girl. You deserve each other."

"Me and the American chick ain't talked about *marrying*, man. Her father ain't *that* liberal. Just having an affair. What would you do if you was me?"

"I'd jump in the Seine," Simeon laughed.

He found himself on his feet, walking slowly, inhaling the cold air, walking with the image of the little girl he had named Lulu Belle. White faces passed him. Lulu Belle. What was he doing in this white world, anyway? Who were these people? What was this strange tearless language they spoke? What could they see through their unscarred eyes?

He did not hear Jinx until she fell in step beside him, breathless from running. "You must be deaf as well as half-blind, Simeon. I called you five times, yelling at the top of my voice.... That sonofabitch is crazy!" The horse-tail of hair cracked over a shoulder.

"Who?"

"Clyde. Always whining, always griping. I wonder why I was crazy enough to marry him. Where you going?"

"Just walking." He did not feel like talking to Jinx.

"Let's have a drink at the Mephisto. I need to calm my nerves."

They ordered rum punch. The well-dressed Martiniquans in the Mephisto were laughing and talking in a Creole dialect. The bright neon lights were garish but somehow fitting and gay, and the place somewhat lifted Simeon out of his mood.

Jinx turned her small light-gray eyes on him. She really was attractive in a crazy sort of way.

"Happy, Simeon?"

"Jinx, let's not start this. Let's not start asking these American Greenwich-Village-intellectual kind of questions. No psychoanalysis and no orgone boxes."

She laughed. "*I've* been psychoanalyzed and I've sat in an orgone box. Fat lot of good it did. God, what a life we had in the States, Simeon. All those New York painters, Christ! All those crazy, fucked-up people. Me, too. Only I wanted to get away from it. Wanted to get away from that wholesale hysteria, relax in Paris."

"I bet you seek out the same kind of people over here, and do the same things."

"More or less. It's a rat race. I met Clyde here, thought that Southern calm might work on me. Woeful day! Can you imagine me taking *that* back to New York with me! He wouldn't fit in. He wants me to go down to Georgia and live with him and his parents. Georgia! Are you kidding! Can you see me in one of these mobs, throwing rocks at little Negro schoolchildren?"

"No, Jinx. That's one place I can't see you," Simeon said more softly.

They ordered a second round of rum punch.

"How do you manage to stay so calm?" Jinx asked.

"Calm? Now?"

"In general. Not just you, but Babe and Benson and Doug, all the Negro Americans. Haven't you noticed it? Look at the difference between the white Americans and the Negroes over here. The whites, except for Lou, are drinking themselves silly, bursting their seams, getting nuttier and nuttier, trying to live like *Tropic of Cancer* or *The Sun Also Rises*. No hold on life. Just spinning like tops and scared to stop. Haven't you noticed it? The Negroes aren't like that. They take it easy, take it slow. They don't drink so much. They seem to have something to occupy themselves, something to think about, something to do—even when they're not doing a damn thing. Haven't you noticed?"

"No." He had not been conscious of it, but now that Jinx said it it seemed true.

"Why do you think it is?" Jinx asked.

"I don't know. Maybe life makes more sense to us."

"That's a funny statement."

"When you have to get out from under the stick, life has a purpose. But life must get pretty senseless if you're the one who's wielding the stick. Unless you're sadistic."

"But none of us over here are stick-wielders."

"It's figurative. Listen, what sense can life have to the average white American with money? What kind of goal can he have? To make more money? Hold on to what he has? That's not much of a goal. But even making money can be some kind of a goal for a poor bugger with a sick wife and nine kids."

Jinx smiled brightly and beckoned to the waiter to bring two more. The drink was rising to their heads. Simeon thought of Lulu Belle. Would Lulu Belle approve of him sitting way over here in this cafe, drinking and passing the time away?

Jinx took Simeon's arm and squeezed it. "I like you, Simeon. One-eyed Simeon. Lord Nelson. Wasn't it Lord Nelson who had a black patch over one eye? I forget."

A couple of Martiniquans waved at Simeon. He smiled and waved back.

"Do you know them?"

"No."

"Why did you wave? Because they have black skins?"

"Yes."

"You feel close to them? Closer than to white Americans?"

"Yes."

"That's strange." She thought about it. "Do you hate white Americans?"

"On the whole, I don't like them very much. I like some of them. A very small minority."

She nodded dreamily. After a while, in a changed, singing voice, Jinx said, "Simeon..."

"Yes."

"Where's Maria?"

"At acting school."

"Nobody's in your apartment?"

"No."

"I'm thirsty. Do you have any...whisky in your apartment?"

"No."

"Any cognac?"

"No."

"Any rum or beer?"

"No."

"Simeon, let's go to your apartment and drink water."

He laughed. "Jinx, I've got whisky, gin, cognac, rum, beer, calvados, Pernod, Cinzano, Martini, wine and saki in my apartment. But let's not drink any."

"Why not?"

"I'm not thirsty."

She pouted a moment, but her gray eyes were amused. "Simeon. How come you don't want to make love to me?"

"Because, A, I'm very happy with Maria. B, I try to avoid screwing married women. C, You sleep with everybody anyway, so one more or less won't matter very much. And D, I don't want to sleep with you."

"Why?"

"Because I think you're hysterical. I don't think you enjoy it, anyway."

She looked at him, startled. For a moment, she seemed

lost for words. Finally, almost in a whisper, she said, "Those are the truest words you've ever spoken."

For a long moment they sat in embarrassed silence. Then Jinx said in a flat, tired voice, "You know, I was married before, in the States. To a sergeant in the Marine Corps. A big, handsome man, a man women fell all over themselves for. Don Juan. I castrated that man. Sliced it off slick as a whisker. Psychologically, not physically. I was never satisfied, I was always tied in knots whenever he made love to me, so nothing happened. Nothing, nothing, I was going crazy. How many women are there like me?"

"A lot."

"So I took it out on him. I told him he wasn't a man, that all the others I'd ever known had made me feel something. I took lovers, and I was frozen with them, too, but I told him that *they* had been *men*. I castrated him. So help me God. He reached the point where he couldn't do a thing. I ridiculed him. He hated me. So one night, when we were in bed, he tried to kill me. I was ridiculing him, and suddenly he put his hands around my neck and began strangling me. He was trying to kill me, no mistake, but I managed somehow to scream. The neighbors came charging in and dragged him off me. It was horrible. You should have seen the hatred on his face. So I left him. It was the best thing for both of us, especially for him; what else could we do? We got a divorce. Mental cruelty!" She laughed.

Then she shuddered slightly. "You know what's horrible? I did the same thing to every man who was crazy enough to fall for me since. And I've done it to Clyde. He didn't drink so much before, it's me who drove him to it."

Simeon whistled softly. "Poor guy. Poor Jinx, too."

"It's awful. I can't help myself. What should I do?"

"I don't know, Jinx. See a doctor."

"I've *seen* doctors."

"I don't know. One day, just like that, the breakthrough will come. You know what I mean?"

"It'll never come. It's awful. Awful. I don't know what to do. I'm going nuts."

3

Poor Jinx, he thought, when they separated later. She walked slowly back toward the Tournon. Simeon shook his head. That girl had problems! But then Lulu Belle came back to him. The problems were worlds apart.

He ran across Clyde, who was hurrying along the street looking haggard and nervous. He had been drinking.

"Where'd you leave her?" he asked Simeon.

"Who?"

"Jinx. I saw her run up the street and join you."

"She just went back to the Tournon."

Clyde hesitated. He was unsteady on his feet and seemed close to tears.

"That wasn't very nice of you, Simeon."

"What?"

"Screwing my wife. I know she screws everybody. But I thought you were a friend."

Simeon stared at him. "You need a cold shower, old man. What the hell are you talking about?"

"I saw her run off after you. I know how she is. But I thought you were my friend. I even invited you to come see me and my family, down South. A friend."

"I'm not a friend," Simeon said angrily. "For your information, I didn't screw your wife. You stupid white bastards think a black man will jump into any pair of open white legs! Go to hell, you and your wife!"

Clyde was puzzled. "You got it all wrong, Simeon. I—" But Simeon turned and walked off without waiting for him to finish.

Simeon was angry throughout his dinner, and even later as he walked toward Babe's place. He shouldn't let that cracker get on his nerves. Felt a bit sorry for the poor bastard, too. But he shouldn't waste his pity. He thought of Lulu Belle and the hideous white mob. Back home, Clyde might have been in that mob. Lulu Belle wasn't looking for any pity.

The more he thought about the little girl with the upright head, the more disgusted he felt with himself. He was over here, comfortable in Paris, leaving the *fighting* to the little Lulu Belles! Would *he* have walked through that mob? Perhaps. But it was easy to say perhaps, way over here.

Babe was glad to see him.

"How come you're alone?" Simeon asked.

Babe chuckled. "Even the *best* of men need a rest from the ladies from time to time. Settle your rear in that chair, there. How 'bout some whisky?"

Babe had a roaring fire going in the fireplace. Bad weather had now settled on Paris: a cold dampness. Babe had apparently been reading and drinking alone. It suddenly occurred to Simeon that he had rarely been alone with Babe, and that he had never imagined what went through Babe's mind when he was by himself.

"Good stuff," Babe said, holding his whisky glass up to the light. "I like that sometimes. Just sittin' up here, all lazy and cozy-like, sippin' a little whisky from time to time. Just quiet. No jokes, no people. Just from time to time. Know what I mean?"

"Yeah."

"A man can't joke all the time."

"No."

Babe chuckled, heaving his immense body around in the chair. "Joke *some* time, though. Laugh at troubles. White people don't understand that like us. Constipated. A man's gotta laugh."

The fire roared. The room was cozy and warm. Babe took the bottle from the table in the center and poured more whisky into their glasses.

"Seen the papers?" Simeon asked.

"Yeah." He looked thoughtfully into space. "It's a bitch, man. The faces of them kids. Some contrast with the faces of them white people. That's where you see the difference in souls."

He sighed heavily. Simeon realized that it was probably because of the picture of the kids and the mob that Babe was alone.

"You ever think about maybe going back to the States, Babe?"

"Never!" Babe said vehemently.

"I feel kind of . . . guilty, sometimes. Like today seeing the picture of the kids in the newspaper. I get the feeling I ought to be there, too, fighting."

"I know how you feel. But I ain't goin back to the States. The States don't say nothin' to me. I been away from all this racism so long that I wouldn't be able to adjust to it. Probably end up killing somebody or gettin' killed. Naw, I ain't goin back."

"Everybody can't get away."

"First of all, everybody don't *want* to get away. Most Negroes feel that's their country much as the white man's, and they want to stay there. That's their business, more power to 'em. Then, some, a few, want to get away and can't afford it. They'd leave if they could afford it. I hope the others that want to come will be able to afford it one day, too.... But don't get no idealistic pictures. Most Negroes are as attached to their television sets and cars as the white people, and they wouldn't like living here."

"But the fight. Don't you think we should be in the fight?"

"Depends what the fight is for. I'ma tellin' you, if we was like the Algerians, and was fighting to free *our* country and drive the white folks out—just like in a colony—well, then, I wouldn't be here. I'd be in that fight. But fight for what? For integration? Man, I don't *want* to be integrated! I don't want to be dissolved into that great big messed-up white society there. I feel like the Black Muslims on that score."

"We don't fight to *dissolve*. We fight for the same rights, voting, education, good jobs..."

"That's the same thing. *Integration*, that's the word, no matter how you put it. Look, I can't do things out of my head, I got to do them out of my heart. Well, listen then: if I was in America, I wouldn't do a thing. I'd curl up and die, like the Indians. That's what I found happening to me before I left. I was an official of the NAACP. We was fighting for integration, integration. Get colored folks into schools, get 'em jobs, get 'em the vote. But I found something wasn't ticking right in my emotions. I sat down and tried to figure out what it was. And I discovered it.

"The thing was that I didn't like them white people, they was my *enemies*. Not all of them, but most. Look at them screaming white hyenas in that picture in the papers today.

You want to integrate with *that?* They was my enemies, there was a fight on, a long war been going on since they took the first slave there, but what kinda war was that when your aim was to be *integrated* into the enemy!... Naw, man. In the NAACP, I had been goin' around making speeches on brotherhood and all that, trying to force them people to *respect* us, to *like* us, to *understand* us. That's what it amounted to. But how could I go on doin' that when I don't even respect or like them—though I understand them all right. Oh, yeah, I understand them. Naw, that fight wasn't for me, and it ain't for me now."

"I still feel guilty."

"Yeah. I feel guilty, too. Lots of folks feel guilty, but I know for me there ain't nothin to do. Just got to live with it, the guilt."

"You'll stay here till you die?"

"Till I die or the French throw me out."

"And if you were thrown out?"

"The world's big, man. There's Africa, Asia, Europe—lots of room. I'm layin some money aside, just in case; you never know. And then the world's gonna see a new phenomenon, with me and some others over here. The Wandering Negro."

Simeon did not sleep that night. He wandered from bar to bar, the face of Lulu Belle always with him. The talk with Babe had not helped. He noticed that the other faces from the picture were there before him, too, the zombie faces, the nightmare faces, leering cold-eyed over Lulu Belle's head. There they were, behind the bottles on the shelf. There they were, in the liquid in the glass. Death masks. He shuddered. It seemed suddenly that he had not moved, that he had run and run in a delirious *chase*, and had fallen exhausted on the spot where he began. The dreams would come back now, he knew that. Faces. He felt an ache in the socket of his eye.

Jazz musicians at Birdland. "Seen the papers?" they asked. They, too, had heard the melody of the child ring clear as a bell against the cacophony of the red-eyed mob. At À la Romance, a softly lighted Spanish bar, Simeon found himself drinking one whisky after another. One of the waitresses slipped up beside him.

"Drowning your troubles, Simeon?"

"I haven't got any troubles," he said.

VIII

I

JOEY THE Drunk walked out of a bar and dropped dead in the street one night early in December.

Joey dead? It was not possible! It was not possible that anyone could die over here!

Simeon had never been very close to the old drunk, but the news came as a terrible shock. Joey dead? They would no longer see him at the bar of the Monaco, or staggering down the rue Monsieur le Prince?

The morning Joey's body was placed on view Simeon decided to go pay his last respects to the old man. Maria brought him a letter from one of his brothers. Mundane things: family, neighbors, the brother's personal life. Thinking of marriage. Working in various Negro organizations (CORE, NAACP). Progress made, obstacles encountered. Simeon put down the letter and lit a cigarette while Maria made coffee. It always made him uneasy to receive letters from home. People always asked: When are you coming back?

"Coffee and kisses," Maria said, bringing a tray to the bed. She kissed him lightly. "I'm going to a cocktail party this afternoon. For the theater group. The movie director will be there, the one I told you about, who thinks I am a good actress. I know you don't want to, but, today, you'll come with me?"

"What time will it be?"

"Begins at four. I must be there a little earlier, help prepare."

"I'm going over for the viewing of Joey's body in the afternoon. I'll come by later, all right?"

"You promise?"

"I promise."

Her face lighted. "Because, you know, I always have the impression you are not interested in the things I do. I want us to share things together. This is the way it should be."

He looked into her weak eyes and kissed her on the cheek.

It was a cold sunny day, and throughout the morning Simeon worked at his easel beside the window while Maria lay in slacks across the bed studying a role. Simeon was not satisfied with his painting: technically it was not bad, but there was no inner drive or inspiration. He kept thinking of Joey.

They lunched alone, and afterward Simeon sat before his typewriter. The editors of *He-Man* had written: "We're interested in an article on the history of chastity belts." He had doubled up with laughter, wondering where on earth he could find information on such a subject; but at the Bibliothèque Nationale and the Cluny Museum he had been surprised to find all the material he needed. He typed for italics the French proverb "A good name is worth more than a golden belt," then began the article:

Ever since Eve gave her now-famous demonstration of how easily women could be led astray, the Adams of this world have been trying to find ways of keeping their wives—and girl friends—out of the arms of temptation.

It was no use, he could not concentrate. Joey kept barging back into his thoughts.

"I feel restless," he told Maria. "Think I need a change of scene. You coming with me?"

"You go, Simeon," she said, looking up from her script. "I stay, study a while, then must go prepare cocktail party. I see you there."

He sat at the Tournon, drinking chocolate milk. African students at adjoining tables were discussing politics. They were furious at events in the Congo, and had harsh words for Moise Tshombe, the president of Katanga province. They debated the relative merits of Sekou Touré and Modeibo Keita. Some of them believed the Algerian war would bring about the collapse of democratic government in France.

Simeon listened, feeling isolated and futile. The future of these students lay clear before them. They were studying administration, engineering, mathematics. They would afterward go home to their respective countries, where they were desperately needed, and take up posts which were ready for them. They would aid their peoples. Their individual destinies and the destinies of their countries were one. Simeon envied them. He thought of his brother and thought of Babe. And then of Joey's death.

Time to go. The funeral parlor was not far away. At the Boulevard Saint-Michel he saw crowds of people standing on the sidewalk and heard shouts from the street. Several hundred students were marching in a demonstration in favor of peace in Algeria. They carried banners: STOP THE DIRTY WAR, NEGOTIATE IN ALGERIA, JUSTICE FOR THE AL-

GERIAN PEOPLE. They chanted, over and over, one demand: Peace in Algeria! Peace in Algeria! Yes, there was a resistance in France to what was happening in Algeria—an active resistance which was relatively small, but which was there. The students were courageous, for demonstrations were banned, and there would be cracked skulls when they ran into the police lines farther up the street. Some people on the sidewalks applauded and cheered.

The demonstrators passed. Simeon arrived at the funeral parlor and found Babe, Benson, Lou, Jinx, and some other people from the quarter. Everybody was staring at the coffin in an embarrassed silence; Babe and Benson nodded furtively to Simeon.

Joey lay there. Skin ashen and dry, mustache and hair white, hands shriveled, the fingertips indented like deflated toy balloons. Lips compressed, the corners still turned down in the perpetual grimace. Eyes so definitively closed!

Back home in Philadelphia, there had been funerals. Many funerals, with all those relatives. Grandpa. He had been a member of the Elks, and when he died they gave him one of their elaborate funerals.

"I don't wanta go," he had told his mother.

"You gotta go, Simeon; what kind of way is that to be? Grandpa always loved you. You gotta go pay your last respects."

For six hours, a child of ten, he had sat with the family on the front row of the viewing room of the funeral parlor, staring at the coffin in which Grandpa lay. Behind sat friends and members of the Elks and other spectators. Just sitting and watching a corpse. That used to be Grandpa. They were gonna put him in the ground. Simeon had shuddered in icy terror.

The Brother Ruler of the Elks stood up with a gong in

his hand. Mamma had explained it to him: they rang the gong three times, each time calling Grandpa's name, and if Grandpa didn't answer by the third gong they pronounced him dead.

"Andrew!" The chilling gong sounded. People in the room began to sob. Mamma dabbed at her eyes with a handkerchief. "Andrew!" The gong tolled like death and the sobs grew louder. Simeon wanted to run and hide. His mother was crying now; everybody seemed to be crying, and in the rear of the room women began to moan as though they were going to break into a hymn. Simeon became conscious of the stifling odor of the flowers, the choking quality of that odor, and he was sure that he would never be able to bear smelling a flower again. He stared in horror at his grandfather, waiting breathless for the third gong, as though he expected the old once-brown man, now gray, to rise up out of the hideous slippery satin lining of the coffin and answer to his name. *"Andrew!"* The gong sounded for the third and final time, the sobs in the room melted into shrieks, and the Brother Ruler said, "I now pronounce you dead."

Sister Johnson stood up and replaced the Brother Ruler beside the coffin. She began the funeral poem of the Elks, "Thanatopsis": "To him who in the love of Nature holds / Communion with her visible form, she speak / A various language...." Baleful poem. Simeon wanted to cry but no tears came; he wanted to run and hide.

> ...The gay will laugh
> When thou art gone,
> The solemn brood of care
> Plod on, and each one as before will chase
> His favorite phantom; yet all these shall leave

Their mirth and their employments, and shall come,
And make their beds with thee.

Simeon turned from Joey's coffin. He was close to tears and did not know why. Images whirled through his mind: the African students, the Algerians, his brother, Lulu Belle, the French demonstrating in the street. Joey was dead; he was alive. But just how alive was he?

Babe and Benson were leaving. They beckoned for Simeon to come with them, but he shook his head. He stayed on for a while. Then he left by himself.

2

He did not want to go to the cocktail party, but he had promised Maria. She was pleased when she saw him, and introduced him to everyone, including the movie director.

Simeon felt depressed, standing in the brightly lighted room with the cocktail glass in his hand, listening to the well-dressed guests discuss plays, actors and critics.

"Yes, I like Claudel," Maria was saying in French, "but I don't understand him very well." Her French was much better than her English.

Maria and her friends tried to draw Simeon into their conversations, but he could not make the effort. Drawing Maria aside he said, "I've just come from seeing Joey, sweetheart. I'm not much in the mood for parties. Do you understand?"

She was disappointed. "You want to leave."

"Yes."

"It's all right. You'll come with me another time."

"Yes."

The cold air felt good on his face. He walked straight home, avoiding the cafés. Ahmed was standing in the doorway of the building where he lived.

"I've been looking for you. I wanted to talk to you. Do you have a minute?"

"Sure, come upstairs."

"No, I'd rather walk."

They started walking toward the Seine. Ahmed was very grave but still rather diffident. "I wanted to say good-by, Simeon. I'll be back eventually, and I'll look you up. Listen; two things. Hossein's been arrested and we've had word through the grapevine that he's been tortured. He's being shipped to a concentration camp in Algeria. And there's something else. My brother's been killed, fighting French troops in the Kabylia Mountains."

"Ahmed!" The words hit Simeon as hard as though the brother had been his own. He put a hand on Ahmed's shoulder and wanted to say something, but he did not know what to say. Ahmed's brother dead. Joey dead. "Ahmed, I'm so sorry."

Ahmed made a helpless gesture. "I've had enough of being a student. That's what I came to tell you. You understand me? I can't just sit by, comfortable, while the others take the hard blows. So I'm leaving."

There was a catch in Simeon's voice. "Where are you going?" He knew the answer.

"To Algeria."

Simeon's world was flying to pieces. He could not imagine Paris without Ahmed. He had grown very fond of his soft-smiling, quiet friend, who in so many ways was like himself. Ahmed turned suddenly and embraced Simeon, kissing him affectionately on both cheeks.

"Listen, I don't have any more time. I've got to rush. I wanted to say good-by to you, Simeon."

"Don't you have a minute?" Simeon asked anxiously, feeling that a part of himself was about to vanish into the night.

"Not even a minute, Simeon." He smiled apologetically. "Once you make up your mind, the FLN arranges things in a hurry. Take care of yourself. Remember me. Remember us."

He clasped Simeon's hand firmly, then turned and walked off. Simeon watched him go away, feeling numb, futile and old. At a corner, Ahmed turned and waved to him, then disappeared.

Simeon walked wearily toward his apartment. It was very cold and damp. West Indians were talking with animation in the Mephisto. A group of drunks from the foreign colony walked singing up the rue de Tournon.

"Simeon."

It was Clyde, walking beside him. The Southerner was drunk and his eyes were red from drink or from tears.

"Simeon, Jinx left me. Ran off with a painter from Montparnasse. Took the kid with her."

Simeon was tired. "Life's tough all over," he said.

Clyde sobbed. "I don't know what I'm gonna do. Christ, I don't know what I'm gonna do! I love her, Simeon."

Simeon shoved sympathy from his mind and feelings. He could not help anyone, not even himself. He remembered with a wry smile something he had told himself as a child, staring in a mirror at the new black patch: "I'll be a great man someday."

PART THREE

The Brother

I

I

FRENCH and American specialists were to operate on Maria's eyes at the American Hospital early in the new year. Maria was calm as the date approached, and spoke rarely of the operation.

"Are you afraid?" he asked her once.

"Not of what you think."

But the night before the operation she lay quietly in his arms and he could feel her body tremble.

After a while she turned on her back, her head on his lap, and stared at the ceiling. She was outwardly calm again. But she whispered, "If it doesn't work. If I'm blind——"

He concealed his fears from her, as she generally concealed hers from him, but he thought about it. If she became blind, he would take care of her. He would wait on her hand and foot, feed her, wash her. His one eye would see for both of them. But she would not become blind.

He took her by taxi to the hospital. A doctor told Simeon, "We think everything will be all right." Simeon did not trust the professional optimism of doctors. For one crazy moment he thought: Suppose the doctors were racists! Suppose they didn't like the idea of Maria being with a black man. Would they go so far as to...?

They operated on Maria early on the second day. "Well, we've done all we can," the doctor told Simeon. "We'll have to wait until the bandages come off to know the result."

"How long will that be?"

"Five days."

Five lifetimes, five centuries. Simeon spent every afternoon sitting with Maria in her room. She spoke little, though from time to time she stretched out her hand to find his. She sat erect, the pillows propped behind her lovely shoulders, occasionally giving Simeon a melancholy smile as he talked, trying to sound casual. When he stopped talking, their silent communication had never been more profound. Simeon felt more sure than ever of his love for her, and sensed that she had come very close to saying that she loved him.

One day she said, "Remember what I told you? That the blind Maria is best?"

"I remember. And it's not true."

"It is true," she said softly.

Evenings, he could not sleep. He could not even bring himself to go home to the apartment before dawn. He did not feel like talking to anyone. When he sat in bars, he kept cold sober. From time to time he thought of Ahmed, wondering what had become of him. It was more than two months he had been gone, now. And Hossein. Simeon imagined himself on an Algerian mountain fighting alongside Ahmed. Then he imagined himself in Angola fighting with the nationalists. Or in the Congo aiding the imprisoned prime minister Patrice Lumumba. Then he returned with an ache to reality. Maria.

Before the day Maria's bandages were to be removed he sat up all night in a café, drinking coffee. Unshaven and exhausted, he arrived at the hospital just after dawn. The nurses were sympathetic; they sat him in the waiting room and told him, "The bandages will be removed at eleven o'clock."

Simeon stared at the clock, wondering how he would manage to stay alive until eleven. But he dozed in the chair and dreamed that an old blind woman crossing a street was almost hit by an automobile. Simeon took her hand and led her to a pavement. An old woman with a doorknob nose and rough yellowish skin. She was hungry. He took her to a restaurant and ordered for her. She could not see the plate, so he cut the meat for her. She had been blinded by flying glass, she told him. He felt strange, talking to a blind woman. He wanted to say something, felt hesitant about what he wanted to say, but he said it: "I'm . . . also blind. In one eye only."

He felt ridiculous. She said, "One eye? Well, that ain't so bad."

"No, that's not so bad."

"You develop the other eye."

"That's it," he said.

He woke again at precisely five minutes before eleven. He sat bolt upright. A nurse came into the room.

"The bandages are off. You can go in now." She smiled. "The operation was successful."

Simeon jumped up, his face radiant, and ran to Maria's room. She was sitting up in the bed with a calm smile. Her body gave way softly in his arms. "Baby, baby, baby," he whispered. She bit his ear.

"Can I have a cigarette?"

She inhaled slowly, leaning back against the pillows, looking at him with a tired smile. Strangely, in this moment of triumph, the sad quality he had noticed in her voice was now in her face. She was pale and thin and somewhat drawn. Sitting on the edge of the bed, he inspected her eyes: they seemed both darker and sharper than before. She had combed her black hair and put on lipstick before telling the nurse to let him come in. Her handsome round shoulders showed through the frills of her nightgown.

"How do you feel?" he asked.

"Tired."

"And happy?"

She paused for a moment before replying. "Yes." After a while, she said, "It's crazy, but I'm afraid. I don't know of what."

"No, we'll celebrate. We'll take a trip, a vacation, like a honeymoon."

"That will be good. Yes, let's go away."

2

Corsica was cloudy and chilly, but Maria swam in the sea all the same. She dove and flipped and turned in the water like a porpoise while Simeon watched her admiringly from the beach. He was a poor swimmer, and found the cold and choppy water uninviting. Maria laughed and taunted him: "Come in, you just have to dive, the first shock is the worst." He shook his head, settled comfortably in the sand in a heavy sweater. Not even the Corsicans would brave that water, so he and Maria had the long stretch of beach to themselves.

The Mediterranean was so blue that it seemed unreal. The beach curved gently toward the village of Porto Polo, near the inn where they were staying, and the low hills stood out against the clear sky beyond. Maria's legs shot up into the air as she dived, looking for sea urchins. On the previous day she had caught several squid on a sort of lance, and the cook had served them to Simeon and Maria for dinner.

The Corsicans were hospitable almost to the point of embarrassment. The people and the land were poor, but the residents of Porto Polo often invited Simeon and Maria to their homes for dinner or to drink the strong local bootleg gin. Whenever Simeon and Maria went walking in the hills they were invited by farmers for fresh milk and cakes. Both of them noticed that the Corsicans, even in other villages, took an immediate and special liking to Simeon: they frequently hailed him on the streets or invited him to have drinks with them in cafés. One day, looking at a post card, he discovered why: there was the head of a Negro on the Corsican flag. No one could explain to him why. But the Corsicans apparently identified him with their flag.

"Oursin!" Maria shouted in triumph from the water, holding up a sea urchin. He had never seen her so gay as during the month since they had left Paris. She had reacted slowly to the success of her operation, but gradually its full impact hit her and suddenly it was as though the whole world of vision were new to her. She *saw* everything with added sharpness: the harsh browns and reds and yellows of the hills, the dazzling blue of the sea, the subtle grays and greens in the stones of buildings and houses, the strong character engraved on the faces of the people.

For two full months they vacationed in Corsica. When they left they toured the South of France from Menton to Marseilles, living in hotels, eating in good restaurants, sometimes dancing in night clubs. Simeon even took Maria to a casino, where he felt out of place and where she played more cautiously than when she was at Enghein, knowing it was

Simeon's money she was playing with this time. They were living beyond their means, going deep into his savings, but Simeon did not care. He would write a whole string of articles for *He-Man* when they returned to Paris.

He bought no newspapers. He did not want to know the news. But sometimes, as he sipped an anisette or put his shoes outside his door for the hotel porter to shine, he would think of Ahmed on an Algerian hill and feel a stab of guilt. Or he would see Joey's cold ashen face and hands before him. Or he would hear the shouted insults of the mob at Little Rock. He would push these thoughts away.

But he was apprehensive finally when the vacation ended and they boarded the train for Paris. Back to the teeming city and back to reality.

II

I

THE SUCCESS of the operation had another effect on Maria—it seemed to triple her energy and ambition to become a film actress. Once back in Paris, she threw herself with vigor into the work of her amateur theater group and at the same time began to cultivate her relationship with the movie director and his friends.

She worked hard on a new play her group was preparing, studying her part in the afternoon with the help of Simeon, who read the other roles. He was amazed once more to note that she had real talent. On the director's advice, she hired an *imprésario* who had a photographer make pictures of her in various stages of undress (Simeon disapproved, to Maria's amusement) and who acted as her agent in the launching of her career. One group photograph, in which she was shown in a night club with the director and some of his friends, was published in a film magazine, and finally one of the sexy pictures also appeared.

A scene from the play her amateur group was rehearsing was shown on the French television network, and Simeon, Lou and Babe watched it in a café and were impressed. "I'm on my way!" Maria shouted. A television producer became interested in her and, after a tryout, promised her a small role in a future program.

Simeon was delighted by Maria's new energy and enthusiasm, except that it so often deprived him of her company. She constantly went to the places where she could meet people who might help her—to cocktail parties and to cafés and clubs frequented by film stars. You could not go to these places unescorted or uninvited, so usually she went with her director friend, Vidal.

"You'd like him," she told Simeon, "if you'd get to know him."

"I can't believe he's doing all this for you just out of the goodness of his heart," Simeon said with an exaggerated frown.

"He's doing it because he thinks I have talent, and because he likes little Maria's legs." She laughed.

"That's what I thought!"

"Jealous?"

"Yes."

"Terribly?"

"Yes!"

She laughed with delight and kissed him. "You don't have to worry. He has no black patch. I have nothing to do with men without the black patch anymore."

Except for the fact that Maria was so frequently away, they lived a fairly settled life. Since Ahmed's departure, Simeon rarely saw any of the Algerians he knew, and he made a conscious effort—with only limited success—to think less about "problems." He told himself that the world was what it was, that it was not his fault, and that there was nothing he could do about it. He had Maria "in the skin" as the French said, and he told himself that there was nothing he could do about that, either. He wanted her to be happy—and they had been happy on vacation. It could go on this way. She was right: life was much simpler when you lived for yourself and let the world take care of itself.

But Maria was away from him too often with the director and her friends and Simeon was annoyed that she did not seem to regret these separations.

He said to her one day: "Let's get married."

She hesitated, her dark eyes, no longer hidden by sun glasses, turning on him thoughtfully.

"You would like that?"

He was irritated. "I wouldn't have asked you, otherwise."

She pursed her lips. For a moment it seemed she would not answer. Then she said: "Wait a while. We have time, yes? For the present I want to become a famous actress."

2

Babe gave Simeon a sly glance one Saturday, and said, "Say, man, how'd you like to be a best man? Me and my Swedish Marika are getting married."

Babe and Marika were married in the *mairie* of the Sixth Arondissement in a simple civil ceremony that took exactly three minutes, in the presence of Simeon and Maria, Lou and Betty, Doug and Benson, and a score of other people, most of them Negro musicians. Babe said "*Oui*" to the mayor instead of "I do," feeling ridiculous in the suit and white shirt with stiff collar and dark necktie. Marika, who was nervous, looked very Swedish with her blonde hair, pale, freckled skin and sky-blue eyes.

The wedding party drove afterward up to Montmartre

to the restaurant owned by Leroy Haines, an American Negro who specialized in "down-home" cooking. "Leroy!" "Babe, you old sonofagun!" Haines was almost as big as Babe, and when the two mountains collided in an embrace the tables rattled and the floor trembled. Haines had not accepted any customers, he had reserved the restaurant for Babe and had laid out two long tables with lines of champagne bottles. Turkeys roasted in the kitchen. Babe rolled his small, round eyes. "Ummm. Smells like home." Benson chuckled. "You sound homesick, Babe." Babe frowned, "How you sound!"

They sat around the tables and opened the champagne. Glasses clicked. The musicians were saying:

"So she done ole Babe in!"

"Brought him back alive?"

"How you figure Marika did it?"

"She baited it with *that*."

"Oh, you mean she baited it with *that!*"

Babe said, "That's right, and if she baits it with *that*, she'll *always* catch me!"

Haines brought out the turkeys, green peas, cranberry sauce, mashed potatoes, corn-on-the-cob and wine, and they all dug in. Everybody talked and laughed at once, and the food vanished rapidly. From time to time Haines came in from the kitchen to witness the results of his handiwork.

"Afterwards," he said with a wink, "I'm fixin you folks some apple pie à la mode."

The party was in full swing when Doug brought the news. It was so startling that at first no one really registered it. Doug had got up to go into the kitchen to talk to Haines, and when he returned he seemed dazed as he announced with his heavy drawl:

"Hey, everybody. I just heard it on the radio. Lumumba's dead. They killed him."

Simeon, Babe and Benson exchanged incredulous looks.

"Munongo, the Katangan interior minister announced it."

No one moved or said anything. Every black man in Paris had felt personally *involved*, personally outraged, by the overthrow of the Congolese premier. And they had felt equally concerned by his subsequent arrest.

Simeon felt like weeping and knew that the others felt the same. They had won again, Simeon thought; the non-men, the monsters. He looked at Maria, who was glancing from face to face, not quite understanding what had happened.

The news had ended the party. The musicians tried half-heartedly to bring it to life again, but there was no more laughter.

As they walked out of the restaurant later, Maria squeezed Simeon's hand and smiled at him, as though seeking some kind of reassurance. But he could not smile back.

They bought newspapers, which had already come out with headlines of the news. On the front pages there were photographs of a group of triumphant leaders of the Congo's Katanga province, the enemies of Lumumba, announcing his death to newspaper correspondents. There were smiles on the officials' faces as they gave their report. With the exception of a couple of Belgian advisers, all of the persons in the photographs were black.

As he looked at the photograph, Simeon suddenly started with surprise. He stared at the picture in wonder.

Those faces! Those *black* faces!

III

I

SPRING came late but was warm and beautiful. However, the joy of Paris was fading for Simeon; the Algerian war was doing something terrible to Paris and to France. As the African colonies gained their independence, as the area of French power contracted, a decomposition was setting in—Simeon could sense it all around him.

French extremist newspapers raged. If Guinea was free, if other African countries were winning their freedom, if the French Empire had vanished, then *somebody* was to blame, *somebody* was guilty—the weak governments, traitors inside France, the greedy Americans, the sly British, the plotting Russians: *somebody*. Embittered Army officers, who had never recovered from the shock of the French defeat at Dien-Bien-Phu, panicked as they felt Algeria, their last bastion, slipping from their grasps. The Congo proved that Africans were not ready for independence; the aid given the Algerian revolutionaries by Communist countries proved that France was defending Western Christian Civilization in Algeria.

The poison penetrated further into the people. One of its manifestations was a rash of chauvinism: ultra-right-wing organizations, with strains of anti-Semitism and a white supremist ideology multiplied. Men returned from military service in Algeria calloused and often dehumanized. Embittered European settlers, who had left Tunisia and Morocco after these countries had won their independence, settled in France and insinuated themselves into key positions of French life and politics.

There had been a metamorphosis in the police—or so it seemed to Simeon—during the year since his arrival in Paris. Simeon had never liked police, but the French police had impressed him more favorably than most. Once polite and attentive, now they slouched on street corners with the insolence of power, cigarettes hanging from their lips, occasionally signaling with obscene gestures to young girls who passed by. Simeon learned that this change in the police was not accidental. The police department had been purged of officers who had shown softness in dealing with Algerians in France.

Most depressing of all to Simeon was the seeming indifference of the population to what was happening in Algeria, with the exception of a courageous minority. Everybody knew about the concentration camps and the tortures. Everybody knew about the filthy slums, the *bidonvilles*, in which hundreds of thousands of Algerians in France were obliged to live. But few cared enough to act or even to protest. *Wir sind die kleiner leuter*—"We are little people": this was the expression the Germans had used, Maria told Simeon, to explain why they did nothing to stop the persecution of the Jews. It was also the attitude of most of the French.

But who am I to criticize? Simeon thought, as the spring grew warmer and he passed pleasant days at cafés and nights with Maria. He had surrendered to her. He was leading the kind of life she desired—one of isolation and abdication from problems. But he could not escape a feeling of guilt whenever he read a newspaper, whenever he encountered Algerians on the street, whenever he saw Ben Youssef.

"No news of Ahmed?" he would ask anxiously.

"No. Where he is, he won't have much time to write. He could be dead or alive. That's the way this war is."

"And Hossein?"

"We haven't heard anything from him. I think he's dead."

The foreigners—Simeon among them—lived in a fantasy world, like foam floating on the sea of French society. They were not involved in current realities in France just as they were not involved in what was happening in their native countries.

The expatriates were an incestuous group—Simeon could calculate that such-and-such a girl had slept with nearly every man in the foreign colony, and just how many girls each man had lived with. In the one year Simeon had known them their faces had changed remarkably. Well-washed American, Dutch, English boys who had come to Paris on a lark and innocent girls wanting to taste "freedom" during the interval between dependence on their families and dependence on their husbands now had dark hollows under their eyes and slouched, lifeless bodies. Only those who worked steadily with a minimum of café life survived intact and with some vitality.

Deserted by his wife, Clyde drank from the moment he woke until the moment he went to bed. He went from woman to woman, as though in a desperate search for the affection he had never received from Jinx. He would throw his arms around Simeon whenever they met, and say drunkenly:

"See that girl? Pretty, ain't she? My girl. Hell, I don't need Jinx. Get along fine without Jinx."

"Sure."

"What do I need Jinx for? Man shouldn't stick with one woman anyway, know what I mean? You *d'accord*?"

"Sure, sure."

Babe had settled down in his apartment with Marika and spent his time either chatting in cafés, taking care of his shop or cooking meals for his friends.

Benson lived a bitter and hermetic life with a new Spanish mistress, emerging from his apartment now and then to drink heavily and launch an ironic tirade against the United States in particular and the white world in general. Simeon asked him one day: "Do you ever think you'll get married?"

He shook his head.

"It's a trap," he said. "A goddam trap. Most of the women they got over here are white, and I could never marry a white woman and look at myself in the mirror again. You know, when I was younger in New York I used to run around with some interracial crowds, and my mother told me: 'If you ever marry a white woman, don't bring her here in my house, you hear! You ain't givin' that satisfaction to the white man! He done said it, done said it a million times—that colored men wants his women. Well, dammit, we gonna prove him wrong! He can keep his women. No son of mine gonna insult black womanhood by marrying a white woman and *stay my son*! You hear me?'

"You know, Simeon, I can't get those words out of my mind. Every time I sleep with a white chick I feel guilt, feel that I really hate the woman. I can't marry that."

Simeon said, "Marry a Negro woman, then."

"That's the trouble. I can't do that either. For one thing, being black, she'd remind me of my own pain. And I wouldn't be able to get rid of my hate, I wouldn't be able to hate her like I can hate white women. Then, another thing, I can't marry her because the white man says I *got* to marry a Negro woman! In a way, marrying a Negro woman would be like accepting segregation. It's crazy, but that's the way I feel, I can't help it. I would be staying 'in my place.' Well, dammit, no! I ain't gonna stay in my place! I'm gonna break all the rules. It's only if you break the rules that a Negro can call himself a man."

He stared straight ahead, then said, "Know what the greatest crime of the white Americans is?" he asked.

"What?"

"That those people made us sick. That they made us as sick as they are. Almost. You know that?"

Simeon said, "Some of us."

"*All* of us. Ain't no people can live under that pressure, that humiliation, without becoming sick. Without being twisted, distorted."

Simeon said, "A lot of us. But not everybody, not even most. Those kids at Little Rock aren't sick. The sit-downers aren't sick. All those people who are fighting whatever way they can for equality aren't sick."

Benson shook his head. "I say everybody's sick. The whole country's got to be sick, because it's a sick situation. But the white people are worse than we are. They're the sickest of all."

Doug worked at the American Embassy by day, and divided his time at night between his American "heiress" and the French girl he said he loved. He told Simeon, "I've made up my mind. I'm giving up the heiress. I'm going to marry the French girl, and to hell with a career."

"That's great, Doug," Simeon said, feeling dubious. The next time he saw him, Doug was again unsure.

Harold, the Negro composer they saw rarely, seemed the

healthiest of the lot. He was living in Vienna and came to Paris only on short visits, like Dean Dixon, the American Negro who conducted the Frankfurt Symphony Orchestra.

"My commission is running out and I've almost finished the concerto. I'll be going home soon," Harold said.

"Home?"

"Sure, back to New York. That's the only place I really feel at home."

Harold always amazed Simeon, he rarely thought of problems of race or anything else. He thought, worked, and lived his music.

"That's the only way to be, for an artist," he explained. "Temporary causes and problems are the death of art."

Simeon said, "There are periods when, as a man, you're bound more to a cause than to art."

"Then one shouldn't pretend to be an artist. One should go get a gun and fight. But leave art alone."

2

I'll be out very late. So I'll probably just go to my room, and not come by here," Maria said.

She looked at Simeon guiltily. He sat at his desk in the apartment, trying to write another article for *He-Man*.

"Don't be angry, Simeon."

He looked up. "I'm not angry. But I don't see you much any more."

"But you could come *with* me, darling. I would be so glad." She sounded sincere. Simeon wanted to believe she was sincere.

He shook his head. "No, that's not being with you, not

with all those people around. You go ahead, Baby. But come by tonight." He felt as though he were begging. He detested himself and was furious with her.

"It will be *very* late. You know how these parties are."

"It doesn't matter. I'd like to see you when I wake up in the morning."

"All right."

She closed the door and he sighed, turning back to his typewriter. He could not concentrate. She was slipping away from him. Well, he had anticipated it. In the early spring, Maria had appeared in a new play and, recently, she had had a bit part in a film. And she was going higher. She was completely a woman now, poised, sure of herself, elegantly dressed. She was no longer the lost refugée in Paris; she was a willful handsome woman headed for a very specific goal that did not include Simeon.

He got up from the table. Through the window he looked at the dark night that seemed so alive to his dull spirit. He did not feel like working. He looked at his black patch in the mirror, wondering what he was. People were identified by their occupations, their actions. Did he, then, have no identity? Was he a shadow, a passive observer? He had a feeling of desperation: he wanted to be alive.

Come to Africa, one of the African students had said.

What would I do there?

Work among a people you'd feel close to. Be useful. Be alive.

Perhaps, one day.

But he doubted now that that day would ever come. He could see no future that was different from the present. He was a prisoner of his own inertia and did not feel the strength to break out.

He went downstairs and outside. The air was warm and humid, and many people were in the streets. He heard a loud explosion in the distance: probably another bomb planted by the OAS, the secret organization set up by right-wing terrorists after the failure of the Algiers *Putsch*. In the name of Christian Civilization. People on the street paused a second at the sound of the explosion, then continued on their way. Was the whole country living like Simeon in a state of passivity and indifference?

He passed the cafés. He did not want to drink; that was too easy. A taxi approached, and Simeon hailed it before he quite realized what he was doing. "Champs-Élysées. The Métro Georges-Cinq." A movie. He smiled with disgust.

For ninety minutes he watched a sultry Jeanne Moreau on the screen. But he was not involved here, either. He felt melancholy and lost.

Simeon walked home afterward. Crowds filled the Champs-Élysées. As he came to the Élysées Club, Simeon saw a laughing group of well-dressed people filing out and climbing into sports cars. Maria was among them. Simeon's heart leapt, he stopped short, embarrassed, not wishing to be seen. Maria was walking beside her director friend, Vidal, laughing happily. The director took Maria's arm and helped her into his car.

The line of automobiles moved off. Simeon stood paralyzed on the street. He was sure that there was nothing wrong with what he had seen, that there was no romance between Maria and the director, but his heart was nevertheless twisted with jealousy. Maria had looked so joyful—with an expression he had rarely seen. He no longer felt like walking home, but hailed a taxi, his ears still ringing with the sound of her happy laughter.

IV

MARIA stretched nude between the cool sheets of her bed. Through the wide-open windows she saw a cloudless sky and the dark roof of the Théâtre de France. She sat up, yawning voluptuously, and her first thought was that she was really *an actress*.

This room was her sanctuary; no man had ever slept in the bed with her. She slipped on a robe and went to stand at the window, thinking of the evening before. Vidal had been hilarious. He was a good director, too. Simeon would like him, if he would get to know him. She decided to take a bath at Simeon's apartment in the afternoon, and got dressed quickly because she had a lunch date with Annette, one of her friends in the theater group.

Maria arrived at the café just in time. Annette was a tall, coldly beautiful French girl with perfect features and intelligent eyes. "Vidal wants you to call him later today, Maria. He says it's very important."

"I know. I think it's for the role he was telling us about," Maria said. They spoke in French.

"But you'd have to travel."

"Don't say it as though that were something bad. Nothing would please me more," she replied.

Annette asked, "And your boy friend?"

Maria hesitated. Why hadn't she thought of Simeon herself? She felt guilty. "It would only be for a few weeks. A couple of months at the most."

Annette shrugged. "Two months is a long time. Vidal would like to get you away from Paris, alone with him."

"We wouldn't be alone."

"You know what I mean."

Maria laughed. "There's no danger. I'm a big girl."

They lunched at the Coupole. Actress! Maria felt triumphant. Her role this time would probably be big, the third or perhaps the second supporting female role. She would move upward in the next film. Vidal was interested in her, and through him she would meet other directors. She could already visualize her name on billboards, see her name in newspaper movie columns, her picture in magazines.

Annette said, "Do you ever think of getting married?"

"Sometimes." She thought of Simeon again, and the guilt returned. Did she love him? Had she ever loved anyone, was she capable of love? She was not sure. "You know what I've come to think, Annette? Two persons traveling separate roads meet and marry in order to continue together along a common road. So before you marry you have to know what road you want to follow for the rest of your life, and what road the other person—the husband or the wife—wants to follow. And you have to see whether you can follow the same road."

Annette said, "I, the allegedly cold and cruel Annette, naturally think in this calculating way. But you always struck me as being a romantic type, Maria. So what about love?"

Maria flushed. "You must love, of course. But you must love somebody who follows the same road."

"And if you happen to fall in love with somebody who is not going along your road?"

"Then one of the two must sacrifice."

"Would you sacrifice?"

For the first time, she faced the question squarely. "I don't think I could. I think I would wither up and die."

She left Annette right after lunch and took a bus to Simeon's apartment. He had left a note on his desk that he would be at the library. The talk with Annette had confused Maria and she was glad to be alone for a while. She undressed and went into the bathroom and ran a bath.

A role! The thought came insistently back to her. But was she less interested in acting than in being an actress? Fame, wealth, her name in lights—yes, but most important, that would mean becoming someone else, that person, that legend on the screen. Acting would mean a metamorphosis, it would wipe out the past, destroy memories. There would be no little Jewish girl named Maria whose body had been profaned by a monster in a concentration camp, no Maria who turned her eyes away as her parents went off to a horrible death. There would only be that person walking across a screen, living, loving and hating on the screen.

After bathing, she put on Simeon's robe and slippers and went into the living room. She lay on the Moroccan blanket and looked through the window at the sky, thinking about Simeon. She saw him as tenderness in a world that was cruel and violent. Her body was in the power of his long, gentle hands. He was generous, intelligent, sensitive, but so complicated. Was it all because of his black skin? No, because she herself, a Jew with the horror in her past, made the effort to forget, made the effort to relax and enjoy life. The way he would brood—over a newspaper article, a talk with Babe, a mention of Ahmed. But this was a weakness, to brood passively rather than taking a positive and firm move, she thought.

She walked to the window, enjoying the pressure of Simeon's robe against her skin. An African walked up the street. She lighted a cigarette, wondering why Simeon was taking so long. Then she remembered that she had to call the director.

"Vidal?" The director's voice was excited as he told her the news. "Oh, that's marvelous, Vidal! Yes, oh, yes, I can leave whenever you say."

She hung up the phone, let out a cry, and whirled around the room. Italy! Italy! Then she halted abruptly, hearing the key in the lock. Simeon came in, tall and handsome, walking like someone who owned the world, a king or a prince. She smiled, remembering their first meeting.

"Hello, Baby." He smiled in his usual disarming way. "I'm sorry I'm late."

"Simeon, the director just called. I'm having a big role in a film!"

"Maria!" She flew into his arms and he raised her in the air, swinging her around. "You're a genius, I knew you'd make it."

"I'm going to Italy!" she cried. "That's where the film will be made."

A shadow crossed his face, but Maria did not want to see it, did not want to stop sailing on a cloud of excitement. But she tried to contain her exhilaration.

"It won't be for long, darling. A few weeks, a month at the most."

Simeon made an effort, too, but there was a kind of resignation and finality in the way he sighed, even as he joked, "You behave in Italy!"

"Yes, I'll behave. And I'll write every day."

She suddenly felt that they were playing games, that a

decisive turning had come in their lives. But she did not want to think about it. Italy! And afterward London, Copenhagen, all over the world! To America even, to Hollywood.

V

1

THE VOICE sounded familiar, but at first Simeon did not believe his ears. He turned, startled to see Ahmed running down the street toward him. The two men rushed at each other, held one another at arm's length, incredulous.

Simeon was shocked at the change in Ahmed's physical appearance, or rather at the contrast between Ahmed's appearance and his own. Ahmed's bearing was more erect and proud, his skin was tanned, his once-delicate hands had become rough and calloused. His eyes had lost all their boyish shyness and shone with serene determination. Simeon felt like a sleepwalker next to Ahmed.

They walked to the Boulevard Saint-Germain and into a café where they ordered coffee.

"What brings you back to Paris, Ahmed?"

He smiled and put a finger on his lips. "An errand," he said. "I won't be here long. A couple of months. I wanted to see you. How is everyone? Babe, Benson, and the others?"

Ahmed's glow of physical and psychological health seemed like an indictment to Simeon. "Everyone's fine. Nothing has changed since you left, Ahmed. You walk into a café and continue a conversation you left off the day before."

"The foreign colony is like that. It seems I've been away a

long time. So many things happened in Algeria. The war's almost over; De Gaulle wants to negotiate and we've won. I have thought of you a lot, Simeon."

"Why?" Simeon asked, embarrassed under Ahmed's intense gaze.

"We're so much alike, Simeon, that with a change of circumstances you might have been in Algeria and me here. I tried to imagine what you were doing in Paris, and what I would be doing if I had been you."

"What would you have been doing?"

"Going from café to café, as usual, I suppose."

"That's what I have been doing, and it's not much of a life in the long run."

"No."

Ahmed asked, "Are you still with Maria?"

Was he? What had Kafka said—"The fox does not know that he is already dead as the hounds bay in their kennels?" He replied obliquely. "She's in Italy making a film."

"A movie? That's wonderful. How is she?"

"I think she's fine. I'm not sure. She rarely writes."

Ahmed said nothing. After a moment he said, "Don't let yourself rot away, Simeon."

"Rot?" But Simeon knew what Ahmed meant.

"You know. 'Drifting from café to café.' I told you I thought about you a lot. I thought about myself—and we're similar. I could have rotted away here in Paris; all I had to do was relax and let myself go. Sink into the opium dream. But I'll tell you something. I was on a mountain in the Kabilya region with a group of guerrillas and the French came at us with helicopters and parachutists and we seemed lost, and I suddenly thought of the Paris cafés and I thought of you. I felt then: 'I've never been happier in my life!' You know that?

Never happier. I was active, alive and felt I was happy for the first time in my life."

Simeon sipped the coffee reflectively. "You were pushed into action," he said. "Maybe I need to be pushed, too."

"I know. But if no external push comes, you have to push yourself."

Simeon said impatiently, "I can't just go out and start a war, can I?"

"No. It doesn't have to be a war."

"I know."

Ahmed grinned. "I told you, we're twins." He looked at his watch. "I've got an appointment. Shall we have dinner together tonight? With Henri and Lou, too, if you see them. Did you know that Henri is working with us?"

"Henri?"

Ahmed nodded. "With the FLN. We have a whole network of French people working with us. Not all of them are bastards." He stood up. "Where shall we meet tonight?"

"At Marco's?"

"Good. Eight o'clock."

2

Walking along the street Simeon passed a newsstand and, with an automatic gesture, turned his face away from the headlines. He did not want to know what was happening, but he knew all the same. What was happening in Algeria, in France, in Angola, all over the world.

He went into the Danton Café. "A beer," he told the waiter. A Frenchman sitting at a table next to him looked at his newspaper and shook his head, then looked at Simeon.

"The politicians should all be shot. They want to keep us on the brink of war, blow us up. I say, shoot them all."

Simeon smiled. Politicians. He did not want to think about them, either.

He stared straight ahead and suddenly in his mind saw Maria, as he had first seen her, pounding her hips against the pinball machine. He imagined her staring into a mirror with her moody somber expression, or lying naked on the Moroccan blanket.

He went back to his apartment because there seemed to be no other place to go and found a letter from Maria. Like her others, it described the restaurants, the scenery, the clubs, the monuments. She was happy: she did not need to say it, it rang in her words. She wrote to him out of duty; she did not say it, he could sense it in the tone. *Do it while you're strong.* The meeting with Ahmed had somehow given him strength. He sat at his desk and wrote:

Dear Maria:

I love you but you have a career and your own life to lead; I feel I have another kind of life before me, though I'm not sure what it will be yet. The two can't mix. Dear baby, to make things easier I don't want to see you when you return. I'm packing whatever things of yours are here and having them sent to your room. When you come back, don't come to see me. And don't answer this letter. Let things end like this. I know you understand what I'm talking about. I wish you all the luck in the world. I'm richer because I knew you. All my love.

Simeon

He felt numb as he folded and sealed the letter. He went downstairs to mail it before he changed his mind.

A few days later he received one short letter from Maria: "Darling. I cried when I read your letter. I don't know what to say; I never felt as close to anyone as to you. But, if I am honest, I must say that I was beginning to feel the same thing. We can talk about this in Paris. I won't come specially to see you, but we will run across each other. The film is almost finished and I will come back soon. Love. *Maria.*"

3

Simeon saw Ahmed almost every day. He did not want to think about Maria and dreaded her return. He doubted that, if he saw her, he would be able to resist rushing to her and taking her in his arms. He did not want to think about it. Ahmed would be his salvation.

"Come to dinner tomorrow at Ben Youssef's place," Ahmed said one day. "Two friends of mine, Algerian women, will be there. I'd like you to meet them."

Their names were Djamila and Latifa, and they were the first Moslem women Simeon had ever met. They had dark skin and dark, faintly crinkly hair like the men. Djamila, the younger, was about nineteen; she was short and plump, with a sweet round face, merry eyes, and an unconquerable giggle. Latifa was tall and slender except for her stomach, which was inflated like that of a pregnant woman. She seemed more serious than Djamila. She was about twenty-five.

The women cooked the dinner, a thin peppery lamb stew with green vegetables. They drank apple cider and black coffee.

"I hadn't met any other Moslem women in Paris," Simeon said.

Ahmed said, "Djamila and Latifa are forbidden by the French to return to Algeria. They were just released from prison."

Round-faced Djamila said gaily, "They arrested us for working with the FLN. They don't want to let us back in Algeria because they're afraid we'd start all over again."

"Would you?"

"Of course," she said with the infectious giggle.

The five of them sat around the table in Ben Youssef's room, which was large but sparsely furnished. The two women had cooked the stew on an alcohol stove which they had placed in the unused bidet. Ahmed and Simeon sat on the bed, with Ben Youssef opposite them and the two girls at either end of the table. There was no paper on the splotched plaster walls and no carpet on the floor. Ben Youssef stared into space, seemingly detached from the conversation, which was in French.

Simeon said to the women, "What's this *you-you* wail the papers all talk about, that the Algerian women make whenever there's a demonstration?"

Ahmed replied for them. "It's a sort of war cry. Before the war, it was a wail of greeting or of farewell."

"I'd like to hear it."

Djamila and Latifa looked at each other and burst into shy laughter. They blushed and shook their heads.

"Please. It fascinates me."

Latifa put her hand over her mouth, to hide the double row of gold teeth, and said, laughing. "It's not the right atmosphere. It wouldn't be natural." She glanced at Djamila again, then said, "We'll wash the dishes. Maybe after that."

They washed the dishes in Ben Youssef's washstand, stacking them carefully on a shelf of the clothes closet. From time to time they looked at Simeon, then at each other, and burst into their shy laughter. It was clear that they had not often been in the company of men. They blushed whenever Simeon looked at them, and lowered their eyes. Yet, these were the most emancipated of Moslem women. They had participated actively in a war. They would never wear the veil again.

Suddenly, Djamila raised her head, closed her eyes and began a slow, eery, low-pitched wail that sounded like a series of *you-you-you-you-you*. Latifa suppressed her laughter, turned her back to the men to hide her embarrassment, and joined Djamila in the chilling cry. It rose steadily in pitch and became steadily more rapid, the girls rocking back and forth and rolling their heads. Their voices sent an icy shiver through Simeon. They broke off abruptly on a very high note, the highest they could reach. Then they burst into laughter again, hiding their faces.

Simeon whistled. "It's bloodcurdling."

"It's to give the men courage," Ahmed said.

Djamila's face lighted. "The parachutists hate it. They can't stand the *you-you* cry, it frightens them. When they come into our neighborhoods and we make the cry they turn pale and point their guns at us and say they will shoot if we don't stop. But we don't stop. And sometimes they shoot."

They sat down again. There was a moment of silence, then Simeon asked Djamila, "Are you married?"

"No. I'm engaged. My parents made the engagement agreement with the parents of my fiancé when he was thirteen years old and I was nine. That was the way engagements were made in Algeria before the Revolution."

"And now?"

"Now, we have the right to choose our own husbands and wives, out of love." She laughed merrily. "I was lucky, I fell in love with my own fiancé. We will be married after the war."

"Where is he now?"

"In prison."

Latifa, turning her grave eyes on Simeon, interjected: "All of the young men are in prison or in the guerrilla forces."

"And you, Latifa? Were you also given a fiancé when you were a child?"

"Yes. He was killed two years ago." She thought a moment, then corrected: "All of the young men are in prison or in the guerrillas or dead."

Ahmed's face set. "One million dead. Out of a population of nine million. Can you imagine it? More than the French or the Americans lost in World War Two."

Latifa nodded slowly. "And the wounded and missing. And the tortured."

Djamila shrugged. "Oh, the torture. Practically everybody's been tortured. Not even worth talking about."

"It's worth talking about," Latifa said, raising her hand almost automatically to cover her gold teeth. "That and the rape."

Ahmed spoke gently, coaxingly, knowing he was touching on a delicate subject. "Tell Simeon about the tortures."

"No!" Latifa said. Neither of the women was smiling now.

"He must know what's happening in Algeria, Latifa. Everybody should know."

"No. I don't want to talk about it. I don't want to think about it."

Ahmed patted Latifa's arm. He turned to Simeon and said, "You should know it. Everybody should know it. Latifa was caught smuggling guns for the FLN. She was raped, of course. But the French officers wanted information about the FLN; they wanted her to betray other members of the FLN, and they tortured her when she refused to answer her questions."

Latifa was pale, staring fixedly at the table. Suddenly she rose, bowed shyly, and ran from the room. Djamila bowed, blushed and followed her. Ahmed explained: "They don't want to be present while I tell you." Then he continued: "They began with the bathtub. They put her in a bathtub filled with soapy water, pushed her head under water until she almost drowned, pulled her out and brought her to. Repeated this about ten times. Then they gave her the hot-and-cold-water treatment, filling the tub with ice-cold water and then scalding-hot water, alternating several times.

"She still didn't talk, so the next day they undressed her again and lay her on her stomach on a cold stone floor and tied her hands behind her. Then two parachutists lifted her from the floor to the level of their waists, one holding her by her feet and the other by her hair. They told her to talk. She refused. So the man holding her hair let go. Her face smashed downward onto the stone floor, her teeth and nose were smashed, her lips were cut to hamburger. The man lifted her by the hair again. 'Talk,' he said. She spat blood into his face. He let go of her head and her face smashed down again.

"She still didn't talk. They gave her time to recover, to think about the pain and time to be able to feel pain again, and then they stripped her naked and beat her with clubs, concentrating on her breasts, elbows and knees. But they saved the best for last. Two soldiers held her arms and two others grabbed her by the ankles and pulled her legs wide open and a paratrooper lieutenant smiled and broke the neck of a champagne bottle and placed the jagged edge against her sex." Simeon winced. "'Talk,' the lieutenant said. Latifa screamed and did not talk. He jammed the ragged-edged bottle into her sex and twisted it inside. She shrieked and fainted. When she came to, they threatened to repeat the whole thing all over again. She talked."

Simeon was trembling uncontrollably in horror. Ahmed spoke with cold fury, his eyes narrowed. "As for Djamila. Her torture was somewhat milder. She was tortured in front of her father and her fiancé, with electrodes. Electricity devices plugged in and applied to the breasts and the sex. Not pleasant, I can assure you. The father, who shut his eyes, could not look; the fiancé, the man now in prison, cried out to be tortured in her place. The torturer turned to the fiancé and smiled: 'Don't worry, *bicot*, your turn will come.'"

Ahmed's face was pale with rage, his lips trembled. Simeon stared at Ahmed, the inhuman images in his mind. Simeon put himself in the place of the women. He was himself in the bathtub, himself before the electrodes. He shut his eyes.

The two women peeked into the room, then entered. Latifa's face was still grave, but Djamila had shrugged off the mood. She let nothing interfere with her good humor. The room was filled with smoke, and she coughed and laughed and said, "Men! Always pipes and cigars and cigarettes."

But the others, including Simeon, could not smile. They sat smoking and staring at the cold coffee until finally Simeon got up to go.

"I'll wait a minute and escort the girls home, they live up the street," Ahmed said.

"Yes." Simeon shook hands with Latifa and Djamila. "I hope we'll see each other again," he said warmly.

"Yes. Ahmed will arrange it."

At the door, Simeon turned to Ahmed, "I don't know what to say. Thank you for the lesson."

Ahmed smiled at him. "Don't fall apart, *mon frère*."

"No."

"By the way, you won't be seeing me out on the streets at night after next week. The government has just decreed a curfew for Algerians. We have to be off the streets by eight o'clock. All our cafés have to close at the same hour."

"It's not possible!"

"Don't you read the newspapers?"

"I . . . didn't see that."

"That's right. Mustn't clutter up the streets, smell up the air for decent Frenchmen. Oh, it's all right for me, with my apartment. But think of the men living four to a room in the slums!"

Simeon looked down the hall. Several Algerians came out of a room and walked down the hall and knocked on another door.

"Don't worry," Ahmed said. "We won't take it lying down. We'll react."

"How?"

"We'll defy them."

"The police will club you down."

"They'll do worse than that. But we have to react." He seemed so much older and more mature than Simeon.

"Good night, Simeon."

"Good night, Ahmed. I'll ring you or drop by your place."

VI

I

ON OCTOBER 1, 1961, the Algerian National Liberation Front (FLN) called on all Algerians living in Paris to go into the streets in the evening and hold a peaceful demonstration against the curfew imposed on them by the French Government. The FLN instructions were that all available men, women and even children were to take part; that they were to parade in orderly fashion, in groups headed by FLN militants; that no one was to carry a weapon, not even a stick or a pocket knife.

It was a cold, damp day. The Paris police prefecture published a communiqué warning that all gatherings on the streets were banned, and that the police would break up any demonstrations that were held. But everyone knew that the Algerians would ignore this warning; everyone knew they would demonstrate anyway; everyone knew there would be fights, riots, and that at the end of the day a number of people would be dead. The faces of Algerians one passed on the street during the day were grim. Sometimes fear could be seen, but always determination. On the faces of the French and the foreigners was something else: varying degrees of guilt and apprehension.

Simeon called at Ahmed's apartment that afternoon, but

his friend was not at home. He had half-expected this. It was clear that Ahmed, along with the entire FLN in Paris, was helping to organize the evening's march. At the Tournon, at the Monaco, at the Danton, in all the cafés where members of the foreign colony met, the demonstration was the center of conversation throughout the day. Most of the English-speaking foreigners intended to go home early and stay indoors.

"You know how them French cops is," Babe said. "When they start swingin' them clubs, they don't see no difference between a demonstrator and a spectator."

"I'm going to take a look all the same," Simeon said.

Early that evening more than thirty thousand Algerians came out of their *bidonvilles* and tumbledown suburbs, out of their crowded hotel rooms and sad cafés, and, by foot, subway, train and bus converged on the centers of Paris. Shopkeepers and salesgirls going to the cinemas on the Grands Boulevards, well-dressed business and professional men and tourists sipping coffee at cafés on the Avenue de l'Opéra, well-fed lovers strolling along the Seine stared in surprise and indignation as the hordes of *bicots* spewed out of their ghettos and took possession of the streets of the capital.

The mass of Algerians, in different groups, converged on key centers: the Grands Boulevards, the Avenue de l'Opéra, the rue du Bac, the Boulevard Saint-Michel, the quais along the Seine. Men in shabby clothes—their "Sunday best"—shuffled along beside women who were often accompanied by their children or held babies in their arms. The men and boys shouted nationalistic slogans: "Long Live the FLN," "Long Live Free Algeria," "Algeria to the Algerians." The Algerian women and girls raised their voices in the chilling wail Simeon had heard from Latifa and Djamila.

Traffic was forced to a standstill. Police rushing to the

scenes struggled to make their way through flocks of honking automobiles. Bystanders fled into cafés or the courtyards of buildings, steel gates slammed down in front of shopwindows, wooden shutters closed over windows of apartments. Those who hated or disliked the Algerians, the majority, cursed them: those who sympathized prayed for the Algerians. The sirens sounded in the distance, the police were on their way.

The confrontations occurred simultaneously in the various parts of the city where the Algerians were concentrated. The police, with long white clubs, converged from side streets and attacked. Theoretically, French police charges were aimed at splitting demonstrations into small pockets, and dispersing the demonstrators; but it was clear that tonight the police were out for blood. While "combat groups" charged, other ranks of police stood behind in each street, blocking escape routes, armed with clubs and submachine guns. The charges split the Algerians into small pockets; each pocket was then surrounded by police who methodically clubbed men, women and children. Simeon saw old men clubbed after they had fallen to the ground, sometimes by five or six policemen at a time, their bodies beaten after the men were dead. In scenes of terrible sadism, Simeon saw pregnant women clubbed in the abdomen, infants snatched from their mothers and hurled to the ground. Along the Seine, police lifted unconscious Algerians from the ground and tossed them into the river.

2

Meanwhile, most of the city slept or went its carefree way. Laughing women and men danced the *touiste* or the *cha-*

cha-cha to candlelight in the Club Privé at Saint-Germain-des-Prés, danced at the Epi-Club, danced at Chez Regine, danced in the ballrooms and cabarets. Old-timers, some of whom had lived through the nightmare of the wartime German Occupation, or even the concentration camps, played cards or dominos or quatre-cents vingt-et-un in the old cafés. Tourists were treated to the specially manufactured charms of "Paris by Night," middle-aged businessmen sent flowers to the nudes of the Folies-Bergères or the Concert Mayol, Marie-Chantal went a-hunting for a prospective wealthy husband or prospective impresario at Le Nuage.

Clyde drank at the Monoco to forget about Jinx, Jinx drank at the Select to forget about herself, Doug made love to his State Department girl, Babe belched after a gigantic meal and joked off a feeling of guilt, Benson lay drunk and bitter in bed with his mistress, and Ahmed lay dead, his head battered to a pulp by police clubs, on the corner of rue du Bac and the Boulevard Saint-Germain.

His body was one of many, dead and wounded which lay sprawled on the street. Curled up like a child on his side, face twisted in a grimace, arms still raised protectively over his head, he looked even more youthful than in life. The police did not know he was dead, and tossed his body, along with the others, into a van. The corpses of more than two hundred Algerians, Ahmed's among them, were to be fished out of the Seine the next day and for days afterward.

3

On a quai near the Pont Neuf, Simeon leaned against the fender of a parked automobile. He did not know what his friends were doing or what had happened to Ahmed or what was happening in the rest of the city. The air here as elsewhere in the city was filled with the screams of women and children. People ran madly, in zigzags and circles, but there was no escape. Suddenly Simeon saw something more brutal than anything he had ever seen before in his life. A few dozen yards away from him a policeman was swinging his club over a woman who was holding a baby. She fell to her knees, bent forward to protect the infant, and the police club kept flying up and down, up and down. Simeon stared, realizing that he was weeping, feeling those blows against his own body. Then suddenly he saw the policeman's face.

He saw it as clearly as though it were only inches from him—that face he knew so well, the face in America he had tried to escape—it was Chris, Mike, their face. The policeman's face was distorted and twisted with the joy of destruction, his eyes narrowed, red dots of excitement on his deathly pale skin.

The face exploded in front of Simeon; and he felt a shrieking dagger of pain in the socket of his missing eye. Simeon did not think, but stumbled forward, almost fainting from the pain in the socket, weaved between the parked cars, and swung his fist into that hated face, with all his strength. Bone rang on bone; he saw the nose flatten and the blood spurt; and then he felt an excruciating pain inside his head and the world blacked out.

He woke to find himself suffocating under a hot crushing mass, with a terrible ache in his head and in the socket of his eye. He became conscious of movement, and gradually he realized that he was in a vehicle, a police van. When he pushed his arms forward to try to open a path to air he realized that he was wedged into a pile of bodies, some squirm-

ing and some inert. The air was thick with stale sweat and
breath, and everyone seemed to be coughing.

The van halted and the bodies were dragged out: bodies
of men and women, some dead, but most wounded and alive.
When Simeon's feet touched ground he found himself in a
clearing outside a gigantic sports stadium. The police were
pulling men out of many other vans while files of CRS riot
police stood on the edges of the clearing and near the vans
with submachine guns. Simeon's head throbbed; when he
touched it, clotted blood came off onto his hand. He adjusted
the patch which had nearly come off his head, then was pushed
roughly into the long line of Algerians being herded into
the stadium. "Get a move on, get a move on!" police shouted
between curses and insults. Simeon stumbled through the
entrance and gasped at what he saw inside: literally thousands
of Algerians sat or sprawled on the floor of the huge stadium,
most of them bleeding from head wounds. He saw no other
recognizable non-Arabs. Simeon and the other newcomers
were shoved out onto the floor where they sat down or lay
on their backs with the others. Most of the Algerians paid
no particular attention to Simeon, but two or three glanced
at him and smiled faintly, without surprise, "*Salud, frère*," a
man said. *Frère*: brother. Simeon smiled. "*Salud, mon frère.*"

The stadium was humid and cold, the air foul. Women
and children lay among the ever-increasing bodies, and their
mounting *you-you* cry echoed from the high-domed ceiling
of the room. Those of the men who were not wounded sat
cross-legged, staring straight ahead of them. Hundreds of
police were everywhere in the room, pointing their guns
menacingly. The moans of the wounded mingled with the
general murmur of voices. There was a stutter of static
and then a hollow voice blared from loudspeakers and the

Algerians quieted down to listen. The voice said the Algerians would remain in the stadium until room had been found for them in prisons, hospitals or camps in France; it added that the agitators among them would be sent back to their "*douars* of origin"—to the concentration camps of the Algerian regions in which they had been born.

Simeon lay on his back and closed his eye tight against the pain. What would happen to him? He did not care. For the first time in a long while he felt reasonably at peace with his conscience. Had his attack on the policeman been a deliberate act of courage, or the result of momentary fury and hallucination. That didn't matter; what mattered was that he had struck at the face.

The pain in his eye had diminished somewhat, and before dropping off to sleep he thought: the face of the French cop, the face of Chris, of Mike, of the sailor, the face of the Nazi torturer at Buchenwald and Dachau, the face of the hysterical mob at Little Rock, the face of the Afrikaner bigot and the Portuguese butcher in Angola, and, yes, the black faces of Lumumba's murderers—they were all the same face. Wherever this face was found, it was his enemy; and whoever feared, or suffered from, or fought against this face was his brother.

4

Simeon woke in the early morning, stiff, aching and cold, his head throbbing. An old Algerian with a beard waved to him and he waved back. Most of the Algerians were already awake and talking in Arabic among themselves. Police with guns slung over their shoulders passed among them, serving a watery black liquid and chunks of dry bread.

The loudspeaker blared: "Stand up." They divided the men into small groups which they placed in designated parts of the stadium and began calling them individually into rooms or to desks that had been lined up along the walls. Simeon was in a group of some two hundred men and women who were seated in a corner of the room. A man next to Simeon smiled and spoke to him in Arabic. Simeon said in French, "I don't speak Arabic."

"Are you African?"

"No. American."

The man pursed his lips and arched his brows in surprise. For a moment, he seemed skeptical. Then he said, "Good."

They sat for hours on the damp cold floor, changing positions frequently to relieve their aching muscles. From time to time the women raised their voices in the shrill *you-you* wail again. Simeon thought of what Ahmed had told him, of how he had never felt as happy as when he found himself with a guerrilla unit fighting against parachutists. Simeon understood now what Ahmed meant.

At around one o'clock police came to them with pots of stiff, lukewarm mashed potatoes with ground meat mixed in it which served as lunch. There were no plates or forks and each man was served in his cupped hands. They all ate hungrily.

A man in civilian clothes wove in and out among the prisoners, looking at the faces. He paused and frowned when he saw Simeon. He walked over to him.

"Are you an Arab?" he asked.

Simeon shook his head. The Algerians looked at him.

"What are you? African?"

Simeon hesitated a moment, then said, "American."

Still frowning, the man turned and walked away. The

Algerians looked at Simeon and smiled. No one said anything. About half an hour later, the civilian returned and said to Simeon, "Come with me."

Simeon made a V-for-victory sign with his fingers to the Algerians of his group, and followed the man across the stadium to the door of a small office. "Wait here a minute." Through the door, Simeon saw a short, stout man, also in civilian clothes, sitting behind a desk questioning three Algerians who were standing. Dried blood was caked in the hair of the Algerians. At another table in the room sat a policeman who was typing notes.

When the Algerians left the room, the civilian said to Simeon, "All right, go in." The stout man looked at Simeon quizzically and said, "Ah, yes." He beckoned him to a chair in front of the desk.

"Your papers."

Simeon handed him his passport and resident's card.

"You're an American. What were you doing in a political demonstration in France?"

"I wasn't in it, I was passing by."

"Why were you arrested?"

"I tried to help a woman with a baby who was being clubbed by a policeman. I got hit on the head from behind, and woke up in a police van on its way here."

The man studied Simeon. His round face was not unpleasant. "You could be expelled from France, you know. You're here as a guest, you have no right to interfere in our politics."

Simeon said nothing. The man looked at his papers again, noting Simeon's name and other details. He looked up at Simeon.

"Promise me you won't interfere in any other demonstrations."

"I should hope there won't have to be any other demonstrations like that."

The man flushed. Realizing that Simeon had avoided making the promise, he said:

"You understand, I know something about your problems. I've been reading in the newspapers about the troubles in the schools. You understand, we like Negroes here, we don't practice racism in France, it's not like the United States. We can understand why you prefer to live here. We wouldn't like to have to expel you."

He waited, and when Simeon did not reply he sighed and handed him his papers. "All right, you can leave."

Simeon was startled. "Leave?"

"That's right, you can go. You're not Algerian. But stay away from trouble that doesn't concern you. Call in the guard outside."

Simeon called the guard. He was astonished to have gotten off so easily, and felt guilty as the guard led him across the stadium floor before the eyes of Algerians. At the exit, the guard said, "You're lucky. See you next time."

"Yes, the next time," Simeon said.

Riot police in steel helmets stood smoking in front of the door, submachine guns dangling under their arms. They looked at Simeon curiously. He put his hand to his throbbing head and walked toward the subway station.

5

It was time to leave Paris. The need to make this painful decision had been nagging at him ever since the riot, two days ago. Now he walked through the Tuilleries on a cool, sunny day. He looked at the gardens, the statues, the pool and the children, the young couples and the old men and women, telling himself that he was perhaps seeing all this for the last time.

On the previous day, Lou had told him about Ahmed's death. Simeon remembered the clubs wielded by sadists, the un-men. He had not been able to say anything, and had only stared out of the window of the Tournon Café. He thought of Ahmed as he had been when they had first talked at the Place de la Contrescarpe—boyish, shy, enthusiastic, sensitive. "We're so much alike, Simeon," Ahmed had said. "With a change of circumstances...."

Where would he go? He asked himself the question though he knew the inevitable answer—even though repugnance swept through him whenever he thought of it. Back to the States—not because he liked it, not because his antipathy to that country and its people had changed, not because he felt any less anger or bitterness or frustration at the mere thought of living there again, but because the Lulubelles were there, America's Algerians were back there, fighting a battle harder than that of any guerrillas in any burnt mountains. Fighting the stone face.

He was walking on the Champs-Élysées now, taking in the crowds, cafes and sounds. As he approached the Élysées Club, he suddenly stopped, seeing Maria step out of a big American automobile, helped by a handsome and elegantly dressed man.

He stood still, weak at the knees, hoping she would not see him, not trusting himself. But her eyes halted on his. They stood still, looking at each other; and then she said something to her companion and rushed to Simeon, throwing her arms around his neck.

"Simeon! How are you?"

"Good, Maria. And you?"

"Good. I'm very good." Her eyes searched his face. "Do I make you sad when I say it?"

"No."

"I'm going to America, Simeon. To Hollywood. That man there by the car is an American director. I have a good role."

"That's wonderful, Maria."

He savored the irony of it. The director was watching them with curiosity. Maria would have to learn, in America, not to embrace black men on the streets.

He felt awkward, seeing the impatience of the director.

"So long, Maria. And good luck."

"Good-by, Simeon. I'll come back to Paris on visits. We can go out together, like old times, yes? You'll still be living in the same place?"

"I suppose so."

"Don't you think you might come back to America someday? On a visit at least?"

"Maybe."

"I'll write. Maybe someday, when I'm famous and rich and have all the things I always wanted—maybe then, Simeon...."

"Maybe then. Good-by, Maria."

She ran to join the director, her long legs flashing in the high-heeled shoes. At the door she turned around, smiled and waved before disappearing into the Élysées Club.

Simeon walked to the French Line office, where he booked steamship passage for his return to the United States.

6

Henri, who was an FLN member but a French patriot nonetheless, wanted Simeon to stay in France. "Once the Algerian war is over, everything in France will be good again."

Simeon shook his head. "It's a long time before things will be good here again. France hasn't really even begun to suffer yet from the things that happened during this war."

Lou was headed for Italy, then back to the United States. "You'd better think it over," he told Simeon. "You've been away so long you may have forgotten what it's like back there."

"I haven't forgotten."

Lou grinned. "Okay. I'll meet you back there, and we'll help to turn the States into a place nobody will want to flee."

Babe joked, but Simeon sensed an uneasiness, and even a smoldering rage, behind his words.

"So you're gonna be a hero. A masochist I call it. Pretentious, too. What good're you gonna do back there? You gonna change things? Become a leader or something?"

"I've got to make the trip, Babe. I've got to find out. You know what I'm talking about."

"I know you're wasting money and part of your own life. For nothing. Your place ain't back there. The fight is being made by the people who're there."

Simeon said nothing. He was certain that Babe knew what he felt. He also knew what Babe was feeling.

Babe shrugged his huge shoulders, staring at him almost accusingly with his tiny, no longer merry eyes.

"Okay, man. It's a silly impulse that won't last long. Write and tell me all about them crackers and phoney liberals and neurotics and McCarthys, man."

"I'll write."

"And when you become an alcoholic or a junky to try to forget about it, or have to lay down on a psychiatrist's couch to get your brains washed so you can adjust to it, or get the jitters and shakes so bad that you can't stand it no more, or nearly land in jail or worse because you try to kill one of them—and you get desperate again for some peace of nerves and of mind and want some juicy barbecued chicken and good red wine, then drop me a line and fly back on the fastest plane you can get. And there'll always be a spare room in my place for you, in case you're broke."

Simeon tried to lift his glass nonchalantly. But his heart sank and for an instant his determination wavered. He laughed however and winked at his friend. "You can count on my being broke."

7

On the eve of sailing, Simeon was surprised at his own calm. Shaving, he stared at his face in the mirror and realized with a shock how much he had aged. He walked into the living room, carrying the razor in his hand. Reaching into the closet, he took out the painting of the face and unrolled it. He did not need the image; the reality had penetrated. He slashed the canvas and threw the strips away.